THE THIEF-TAKER'S APPRENTICE

CHARLIE GARRATT

BUNLACKY PRESS

Copyright © 2025 Charlie Garratt

The right of Charlie Garratt to be identified as the Author of this Work has been asserted by him in accordance with the Copyright, Designs and Patents Act 1988

First published in Great Britain in 2025 by Bunlacky Press

Apart from any use permitted under UK copyright law, this publication may only be reproduced, transmitted or stored, in any form, or by any means, with the prior permission in writing of the publisher. You may not, except with our express written permission, commercially exploit the content of this novel.

This is a work of fiction, though inspired by real historical events and figures. While the setting and some characters are based on historical accuracy, the plot and dialogue are entirely the author's creation. The author has taken certain liberties with historical events and some characters for the purposes of storytelling. Any resemblance to actual persons, living or dead, events, or locales is purely coincidental.

ISBN 978 0 9931784 1 2

OTHER BOOKS BY CHARLIE GARRATT

The Inspector James Given series
  A Shadowed Livery
  A Pretty Folly
  A Patient Man
  Where Every Man
  A Malignant Death

A Handkerchief for Maria

Wild Atlantic Words (Contributor)

All available on Amazon as paperback or eBook

charliegarratt.com
charliegarratt.substack.com

Acknowledgements

No author works alone. We draw inspiration from the people and events around us, and, hopefully, we receive support from our friends and family. I'd like to thank all who've helped in the writing of *The Thief-Taker's Apprentice*.

In particular, I want to thank volunteers at Bridgnorth Museum who guided me in my research, Ann Reader for her helpful insights into the final draft, and to members of Writers on the Edge for their encouragement and eagle-eyed reading of my chapters as they were created.

Most of all, I couldn't have written anything without Ann, my constant companion, my muse, and the source of so much guidance.

This novel is dedicated to Catherine, who I hope would have enjoyed it. She left us before I finished it.

A good soul gone too soon.

One

Bridgnorth, Shropshire, early November 1749

For a moment Sarah thought she might have misheard, a trick played on her mind between dreams. Then, an unmistakable creak on Cliffe House's floorboards told her she was very much awake. The woman's first reaction was to reach for the dagger Aubrey had tucked beside her bed before leaving. It was there, and the carved bone handle gave her nerve in a moment. She was rarely grateful to her husband but whispered a "thank you" for his foresight on this occasion.

Sarah edged from beneath the blankets and checked Hannah still slept, safe in her cot by the wall. The child's cheek felt soft and warm under the mother's fingertip, which did not linger long, to avoid waking the girl. Hannah still did not stir when Sarah tiptoed to the door and pressed an ear against it.

The only light in the room came from the hearth. Coal embers still shone a dull red, even though the flames had died hours earlier. Tonight had been the first time she had asked her maid, Polly, to light a fire this year. Autumn had been mild, though this evening had grown chill, and she had felt the need of it. Sarah felt grateful for the glow cutting through the pitch black. Without it, the magistrate's wife would have been even more fearful.

Her back pushed hard against the wall, feeling comfort in its stern immobility. Hardly breathing, she listened. Leather on wood, muffled, as if in her adjoining dressing room, then nothing. Had the intruder stopped, or moved onto the rug? A drawer slid open, closed, then another. With her mind's eye, Sarah could see the hands moving aside her clothes and her papers. Searching. For what? When the fourth one closed and no noise came from the fifth, she had an inkling.

Her husband travelled to Shrewsbury the previous morning and had planned to stay overnight. Was this him, come back early, unable to find a harlot to share his bed? If it was, why would he sneak into her dressing room? Certainly, a jealous man, despite her never giving him cause, though he'd have no need to search her room in secret. Aubrey had a husband's power to demand access to it whenever he might wish.

If Joseph, the footman, had been in the house, Sarah would have guessed it might be him, she'd never trusted the man. She was sure he would be pleasant to your face and a weasel behind closed doors. But he had left before dark, having begged to spend the night in Swancote with his family. His mother needed all the help she could get, having given birth to yet another child a week ago. This one was the eleventh since Joseph entered this world a little over eighteen years earlier. Sarah had not wanted to be alone overnight, though could see no way she could refuse, so she let him go until first light.

Who else might it be? Catherine Garris, the cook, had been with Sarah since she and Aubrey had set up home together and had always seemed loyal. Sarah could not imagine Mrs Garris being a thief. Polly was in and out of the dressing room all the time, so would have no need to creep about in the middle of the night if she wanted to steal something. The cook, the footman and her maid were the only ones living in the house. All the other servants shared rooms above the stables. There would be a good chance any of those would be discovered and questioned if they tried a nighttime ramble into the house.

Whilst Sarah pondered, the footsteps moved onto the landing, pausing outside her bedroom. The weight of tread now assured her it was a man. She gripped her weapon tight, white-knuckled, ready to strike if the doorknob turned. It did not. Though it seemed an age, she heard only two ticks of the clock before he retreated. Sarah waited a moment, then put her eye to a knothole. The dim light from the hall lantern silhouetted a figure creeping down the stairs.

Emboldened by the dagger growing warm in her fist, Sarah's temptation was to follow. Call him back. Make a challenge. But this would be stupid, and put her daughter, and herself, in danger. Instead, Sarah Beaumont screamed inside, sank to the floor, and waited for the dawn.

Two

Edwin Hare tipped a finger to his forehead when he noticed me crouching to cut roses. 'Morning, Meg, they're looking good.'

'They are sir. Mistress Sarah asked me to gather them for the table. She will be pleased.'

As soon as I closed my mouth, I thought I had gone too far. The man isn't anywhere near as grand as the master. He's a thief-taker who chases all manner of ne'er-do-wells and brings them to justice before my employer. But he *is* a regular visitor. And one who's listened to. If he tells Mr Beaumont I spoke out of turn, I'll be thrashed. Or locked in the shed overnight at the very least. I bowed my head back to my work.

He didn't move off as I'd expected. I squinted up and Mr Hare was grinning. 'Then the magistrate's cook will need to prepare something special to match them. I'll have to wheedle myself an invitation to dinner.'

Now he went on his way, his long shadow stretching ahead of him until he reached the house. A strong rat-a-tat brought Joseph, the footman. I wished

I had Hare's confidence to bang on any man's door and demand entry. All the tradesmen went round the back, but not him.

I wondered if it was his height, for it could not be his station. But I knew men, almost as tall, and they quaked in the presence of rich folk the same as the rest of us. I've often seen Hare in the town, with men listening, nodding, and scratching their chins whenever he spoke. There was something else, like as if he has wisdom and strength denied to most of us. They say even his employer, Mr Perry, the coroner for Shropshire, gives him respect. I know, for a fact, my master does. I would wager our King George himself would accept his good counsel.

Joseph looked my way when Mr Hare went inside, then blew me a kiss, bold as you like. I didn't return it; in case the Master or Mistress were watching from a window. They'd issued clear instructions there'd to be no relationships between the male and female servants. Mr Beaumont would sack me for certain, and though I've my hopes, I need this job. Despite this, I winked. I don't know why, a footman won't get me to where I want to go in this life. He's a fetching enough man, is Joseph, with a ready grin, and that neat little moustache, though very forward. Sadly, he mightn't be the brightest button in the sewing box. On top, I find his habit of screwing up his eyes when thinking is very off-putting. I can't see him rising higher in the years to come.

Is it wrong for a gardener to have ambition? I don't think so, but it feels disrespectful to my dad to want to be something better than he is. I know I wouldn't even have *this* job if I still had a brother. He'd have taken it, for certain, when Mr Beaumont asked Dad to find a new under-gardener to train.

Joseph sniggered at his game. He pushed past Hare, begging his pardon when the visitor stepped out of his way with a curse. At a full three paces across, the servant could have passed without disturbing Edwin. The lad's haste, with his mind still on Meg, had made him clumsy. The footman's knock at the sitting room door received an emphatic order to enter.

Joseph bowed his head when he swung the door open, the smile gone from his cheeks. 'Mr Hare to see you, sir. Said you would be expecting him.'

Aubrey Beaumont, magistrate, landowner and one of the most influential men in Bridgnorth, lifted his hooded eyes from his papers. 'Indeed. Thank you, Joseph.' He stood and thrust out a well-practised hand. 'Welcome, Hare. Come in and take a seat.'

Edwin had never seen him wear a wig, not even on the bench. The greasy hair and dark stubble told of a man who cared little for his appearance, nor of the opinions of others. It was clear Beaumont believed his wealth and his young wife made all the impression he needed.

Both the magistrate and his guest knew the boundaries of their relationship. They took the modest chairs either side of the desk, not the plush ones overlooking the lawn and orchard. Beaumont reserved these for evening relaxation, for important customers, and for his friends from Shropshire society. His stable of land and river transport shipped out a quarter of all the iron, bricks, and pottery from the county. They shipped in a similar proportion of sugar, tobacco, and wines from across the world. Hare knew him to be a shrewd, some would say ruthless, merchant. Always ready to squeeze an extra guinea to add to his considerable fortune.

Edwin had been in the room many times. He never ceased to marvel at how it was larger than his whole home. The merest fraction of its furnishings would cost many years' wages of one of the magistrate's labourers.

Beaumont dismissed his footman, without requesting refreshment for his guest. Instead, the magistrate peeled a sheet of paper from a neat pile and ran his fingernail down the list. 'I am back from Shrewsbury in the last hour, Hare, and what do I find? Reports of wrongdoing all over the town, that is what I find.

'Five thefts of property in the last week. Four burglaries, all from the better houses in High Town. And the farmer, Charles Tindal, robbed at pistol point as he rode home to Highley. It is becoming worse. To top it all, a prisoner escaped from the gaol last night.'

Hare wanted to say it was only worse for the victims, for him it was, without doubt, better. More demand for his services. He shrugged. 'What do you want me to do about it, Mr Beaumont? Are these people putting up rewards? Are you? If not, then it's no business of mine. I'm sorry for their difficulties, any decent man would be. The rise in crime these nine months since Christmas is alarming. Yet, though it might keep you awake at night, it does not me.'

If Beaumont didn't like what he heard, Hare did not care. The man only held his office due to his wealth, not his knowledge of the law. He didn't even have a strong commitment to uphold it and needed Hare much more than the reverse. The thief-taker's customers would always pay good money to have stolen goods returned, or a debt collected. Only once in a blue moon would the good burgesses of the town put forward a bounty through Aubrey Beaumont. Hare knew the pressure to bring villains to justice was on the magistrate, not on him.

Beaumont's features hardened, then relaxed, his chin resting on interlocking fingers. The discussion had now come down to a negotiation. Every day he made agreements, either with customers or suppliers, and thought himself to be good at it. He would not have expected to ask a favour without bargaining something in return. 'You are saying it's not your business, Hare, but some believe you may be at the back of it. I would not presume to make such a serious accusation, but you must know it is the talk of the coffee houses.'

'Who says such a thing? Bring them forward to accuse me to my face and I'll knock them flat.'

'That may be, but Jonathan Wild is still in people's memories. That scoundrel was born not five leagues from here and you are a thief-taker like him. All know he encouraged his criminal friends to steal from the good folk of London, then turned them in for the rewards. Despicable.'

'But I'm no Jonathan Wild and I will not let you say that I am. He deserved all he got. If you think I'm of the same ilk, then we need to part company. You may not see mine as the most attractive of occupations, but I would not stoop to Wild's level.'

Beaumont held up both his hands. 'Did I say I was accusing you? No. All I meant was other people in Bridgnorth may not know you as well as I do. They might think if you mix with thieves, you must be one. They might also say you have only been here a few years, and they have no knowledge of you before then. To them, you could be anyone.'

Edwin stood, walked to the fireplace, and hawked in the grate. He placed his hands on the mantel and stared into the smoke for a few moments before he answered.

'Then they should mind their own business and keep their beaks out of mine. The good folk of Bridgnorth soon come running when they need my skill, do they not? What is it you, and they, want me to do?'

A self-satisfied smile flickered on the magistrate's face, and he stroked his stubbled chin. This was as much pleasure as reeling in a fine Severn salmon. Or as playing a winning card when gambling with his drinking friends. 'So, you will help? I am sure the townspeople would feel forever in your debt if you were to find who is behind these crimes.'

Hare shook his head and spat out the hook. 'That was a nice try, your honour,' he bowed, 'but not today. Not without a good pile of shillings to make it worth my while.'

Beaumont ripped his list of crime victims in two. 'Then I will bid you good day, Hare. I had hoped to prevail on your good will, but I see you have none.'

'Let me ask you a question, Mr Beaumont, if I may. You have a whole fleet of trows plying trade up and down the river below us, do you not?'

'You know I do.'

'And you charge a fair price to transport goods upon them I imagine.'

'I would hope so. What are you getting at?'

'Only this. If I was to bring you a hundred leather hides, or twenty bushels of wool, to take to Gloucester, would you do so for free because we are acquainted?'

'Of course not. That way would be the road to ruin, for me and all my boatmen.'

'Then so it is with me. I may not be as grand as you, and I may not earn as much in a day as you, but I cannot work for nothing.'

'But this is different.'

'No, it isn't. Your income arrives from transporting goods, mine from catching thieves and cut-throats. Ask the victims to club together for a reward or convince your friends on the Council to dig into their deep coffers. Then I can assist. Until that time, I must refuse.'

Edwin didn't mind that Aubrey Beaumont had returned to his ledgers without accompanying him to the door. He hadn't even rung for Joseph to show him out. It was what Edwin wanted. A chance to meet the magistrate's young wife without the hindrance of her husband or a servant in tow.

He had seen Sarah Beaumont at her husband's side in the town, and thought how ill-matched the pair were. The lady always well-dressed and well-featured. The husband thick set, red-faced, and cloaked in worsteds and thick boots. Never the foppery worn by many of his peers. Not even a wig. Despite his grand town house and wealth, anyone would take Aubrey Beaumont to be a farmer, or a country squire at best. Nobody would make the same assumption of his wife. As fine a lady as Bridgnorth had to offer, and, in Edwin's opinion, as pretty a one too.

Edwin had given little thought to what he might say to her if he had the chance. He'd heard rumours the couple may not have a happy marriage, but this didn't mean she'd begin a relationship with someone like him. A man with fewer prospects and much less wealth than her husband. All Edwin knew was that he found her attractive and wanted to meet her.

When he passed the staircase, a vision granted his wish. He almost bumped into Sarah Beaumont. The light from a window gave her blonde locks the halo Edwin already had in his mind's eye. He opened his mouth to speak but she gasped and scurried back up the stairs to disappear round the corner of the landing.

Hare wanted to call her back, effect a proper introduction, and apologise for startling her, but he knew it would not be proper. A raised voice would bring the husband from his room, and this might cause difficulties.

Edwin waited a minute, hoping the lady of the house would reappear. He looked again when he reached the front door. She did not.

If he wished to talk to Sarah Beaumont, he would need to bide his time until the opportunity arose again. With Aubrey Beaumont well out of earshot. The knowledge that they had at least met, even if they had not spoken, put a spring in Edwin's step when he left Cliffe House and strode into the garden.

Three

Two things caught my eye. The first, Mr Hare leaving the house, was hardly unexpected. He had to come out sometime. The other, my mistress peeking down at him from a window, was more surprising. There was no mistaking the look in her eye, nor the flush on her cheeks. My master, Mr Beaumont, wouldn't be too pleased if he found out there was an affection between them. Something to keep close to my chest. Knowledge which would be useful as a lever to move Mr Hare if he didn't offer the favour I wanted.

I abandoned the rose picking I should have been doing and turned my attention to spreading muck on to the bed close by the gate. Mr Hare would be more likely to see me there. If, as I prayed, he spoke to me, I would make my request. Even if he thought me forward, he'd be unlikely to return to speak to the magistrate about it. In my eagerness as my target approached, I missed another figure leaving the house. My master startled me when he stepped from behind a hedge.

The dung on my raised shovel flew straight in Mr

Hare's direction, only missing him by inches as he jumped out of the way. 'Whoa, careful Meg Valentine.'

My master was less inclined to be forgiving. His slap round my head fair rattled my teeth, knocking me to the ground. I cringed, expecting his boot to crunch into my back. It wouldn't be the first time.

Mr Hare came to my rescue. 'Beaumont. Stop, for God's sake. It was an accident.'

I couldn't see Mr Beaumont's face though heard the edge to his voice when he replied. 'Please do not tell me how to treat my own servants, Hare. This girl is a lack-brain and needs to be taught how to behave. I am sure you would be less forgiving if she had hit her target. Doubtless you would demand I pay for the cleaning of your clothes.'

The thief-taker stayed quiet for a moment, and I imagined he was considering his next step. The master's words sounded like a challenge. One which Mr Hare wouldn't ignore in other circumstances. His height and clear strength would make it an unfair fight. But he'd be unlikely to enter one with an influential man who could make his life very difficult. He shrugged. 'I would not presume, sir, to guide you in such a thing. I would only ask that you show a little mercy. You are right, if the muck had hit me, I would not have been pleased and may have cuffed the lass myself. But it did not, and there is no harm done. My apologies if I interfered too in too strong a fashion.'

His tone seemed to do the trick, and my master pulled me up by the ear, then stepped round me to face Hare on the path. 'This is the second time today we have crossed words, Hare. I hope it does not signal a deterioration in the good relationship we have held so far. Let us hope that the next time we meet you will be in better humour. And please give further thought to the question I put to you inside. A more positive approach to that matter will, I am sure, assist.' He turned back to me. 'And you, girl, thank this gentleman for his concern for your welfare. Then get back to your work with more concentration and a little less vigour.'

The magistrate nodded his head once more in Mr Hare's direction and walked back towards the house. I burbled a few words of apology and gratitude and prepared to ask for the favour which only he could supply.

Since the first time I saw him visit my master, and when I discovered how he earned his living, I've thought how fine it'd be to be a thief-taker. To spend my days poking my nose into people's lives and have them reward me for it. Before I could succeed in such a venture though, I knew I'd need Mr Hare's help to teach me how it's done. The kind words he'd given me earlier had filled me with hope that he may agree. The frown which now appeared on his face once my master left us, told me not to ask today.

Without speaking further, he swung away, pulled down his hat brim and strode past me. He left the gate squeaking on its hinges as he turned into the lane. Perhaps I'd need my little piece of information about what I'd seen after all.

I returned to my roses, snipping the fresh red buds,

as my father had shown me. When there were enough in the basket I took it round to the kitchen. To my surprise, Joseph, rather than Cook, popped his head out when I knocked.

He smiled and almost doubled in a deep bow. 'Why Miss Valentine, how lovely to see you again so soon. What can I do for you?'

The tease in his voice made the blood rise through my cheeks. I thrust out the basket. 'Th..these are for the Mistress. Sh..she asked me to pick them for the table.'

The footman lifted a bud and sniffed. 'Lovely. If I pop them on the hearth, they will open nice by dinner time.' He grinned again. 'Is there anything else I can help you with?'

Still red-faced, I scurried back to my loft above the stables, leaving him at the door laughing.

Sarah Beaumont felt distracted. Her initial fear of the nighttime visitor had soon turned to anger at herself for not confronting him. Aubrey had arrived home in the morning when he'd said he would. So, unless it was an elaborate plan, he hadn't been the intruder. Whoever it was, had stolen some precious things. Not precious in their monetary value, but in what they meant to her. A link to times lost. Through the sleepless night, the fear had returned. This time it was not the physical presence of the thief, but what he might do with what he had stolen. If he passed the items to Aubrey, her time here at Cliffe House would be over.

On top of this, the encounter with the thief-taker in her hall had made her head spin even more. A handsome man. Tall and muscular with no sign of running to fat like Aubrey. His russet hair, rare around Shropshire, and the white scar along his chin hinted at an interesting past life. She wished to know more of him.

Her attempts to sit reading in her room had not dispelled her disquiet. Twice, at lunch, her husband had asked if she was well. Sarah made an excuse that she had experienced a minor difficulty with her embroidery, and this had taken her mind elsewhere.

When Aubrey returned to his room, she had taken her daughter for a walk in the garden to try to clear her head. They walked from the front of the house, with its neat, clipped lawns and hedges, round the side under the shady trees and into the back. Here the smell of baking hung over the path past the kitchen, only fading when they reached the orchard. The sight of apples, red, ripe, and waiting to be picked, cheered Sarah a little. She reached up and pulled one from a low branch, sniffed its freshness and bit into the crisp, sweet, flesh. She smiled as she wiped a dribble of juice from her chin and watched Hannah toddling along the path. The child, as children do, chuckled at the wonders of the world around her. The two made their way through a gate into a walled area bordered by shrubs and autumn colour. In this moment, Sarah forgot her concerns.

Then her daughter stopped and pulled something

from beneath a small round stone on the bench. She held her tiny hand towards Sarah.

Sarah bent to take the scrap of paper from Hannah's fingers. 'What do you have there, chicken?' A note, folded in four. Grubby and the cheapest quality.

Sarah looked around. Was whoever had left it still somewhere in the garden? She could see no-one but was sure there'd been nothing on the bench the previous afternoon. Unfolding the paper, Sarah clapped a hand to her mouth when she read the words. All night she had expected a message of some kind, but the hard realisation of her situation now almost overwhelmed her. She slumped down on the bench, pulling Hannah close, and re-read the note.

Madam. Some things of yours have come into my hands. You want them back. I will be in touch.

Clumsy and no demands, other than to wait. The writer knew something of her, that was obvious. At least enough to be certain where she sat and where no-one else would be likely to find the note. Yet he, or she, had not addressed Sarah by name. Did this suggest deference, like a servant, or caution, in case another *did* find it? There would be little point in attempting extortion if someone else became aware Sarah had matters worth hiding.

Sarah folded the note again and slipped it into her sleeve. She rose and took Hannah's hand, leading the girl, still skipping and jumping, along the path from the walled garden back into the house.

A couple of days came and went, with me watching the gate, hoping to catch Mr Hare when he returned. He didn't. It'd been quite easy to keep my eyes peeled. As winter approaches, there's much less work in the garden. Most flowers are at the end of their season and summer vegetables have passed. This, and shorter days, mean I've time to myself I don't have at the peak of the year, though there's still plenty of work to do. My father, as head man, keeps me busy, that's for sure.

To keep my lookout, I wandered through the front garden, pretending to check this or that. From there I could see the lane passing the front of the property and the main gate leading from it. There's another entrance at the side, but I knew Mr Hare wouldn't usually come through that one. He sees himself a class above the servants and tradesmen who used it.

After my failed attempt to talk to him, I thought I might convince him I'd be fit to receive his help if I practised the arts I needed. To this end I'd spent my free time over the past days following the movements of others from the household. My first attempts had been pathetic, walking so closely behind they noticed me, and I had to invent an excuse for being in the place. If I lagged behind too far, I lost my target very soon. With practice, I'd become a bit better and when the time came, I was ready to make my plea.

That afternoon, my master sent me on an errand to his boatyard by the river in Low Town. I set off and approached the lane by the side gate that we servants are allowed to use. When I spotted Eric, the son of a neighbour, Tom Dyke, I held back behind a large oak tree which stands there.

The lad, like me, is around seventeen years. He's handsome in a plump kind of a way, and his father's few acres would make him a decent catch for a half-pretty gardener with a little ambition. I decided to follow Eric. If I could discover where he liked to go, and what he liked to do when away from home, I might be able to make good use of this information later if I wanted to talk to him. At least I'd have some more experience to impress the thief-taker.

From the shelter of tree trunk, I watched Eric stride toward the town in the watery afternoon sunshine. I only ventured out when he reached the far end of the lane and was unlikely to notice my movement. Stepping lively when my quarry turned the corner, I soon caught up enough to see the street he had taken. His destination should have been obvious had I thought about it. The market. He sauntered amongst the goods on display, lifting a tool here, an apple there, and I saw nothing which would help me grab his attention the next time we spoke. I was about to leave when I felt a hand on my shoulder.

'Meg, what are you up to?' It was Mr Hare's voice. I turned and he winked then nodded in Eric's direction. 'Good looking young lad, that one. Might be a bit above your station though, eh?'

The blood rose in my cheeks. 'I was following him, that's all.'

'What?'

His laugh made me blush all the more. 'I ... I mean I was practising.'

'Ay, but practising what? You can't go following men about the streets you know, my girl. Whatever would your mother say? Or that lad's mother for that matter.'

My tormentor saw how embarrassed I was and apologised. He then took my elbow. 'Come over to the wall, Meg. I want a word.'

By the alehouse and the grain store we stood in the shadows, where we couldn't be seen.

'Can I ask you, Meg, does the magistrate beat you often like he did when was there?' I said nothing, though the memory of the times he'd punished me stung almost as much as when his boots or stick laid into me. 'Come on, you can tell me, miss. Does he beat you often?'

'I shouldn't say, Mr Hare, sir.'

'From that, I take it he does. Am I right?'

I nodded.

'And do you deserve it?'

'If the master thinks I do then I must, mustn't I, sir?'

'There are men in this world, Meg, who take pleasure from the hurting of others, but you're good to be loyal to Mr Beaumont.' He leant back against the wall and peered down at me. 'Now then, what are you up to following Tom Dyke's boy?'

I hesitated before replying. 'I want to be like you, sir.'

'Like me? Do I go following young men about the

town?'

'You must sometimes, sir. How would you catch thieves otherwise?'

'Ah. So, you want to be a thief-taker?'

Anyone watching would have wondered why such a huge grin appeared on my face, but I couldn't help myself.

'I do, sir. Very much. Can you teach me?'

'Why should I?'

The question stopped me in my tracks. I'd thought he'd have been happy to take some help. I blurted out the first words which came to me.

'You need an assistant. You know you do. Everyone says there's crime everywhere. More than ever these days. You can't do it all yourself.'

'An assistant? I have no need for, nor money for, an assistant.'

'Money? I had not thought of payment. Not yet awhile anyway.'

'That aside, thief-taking is no line of work for a woman, is it?'

I stopped myself from screaming. 'They'd say the same of being a gardener and I am the only female one in Bridgnorth, but Dad says I'm the best. After him, of course. If you show me your tricks, I'll do the jobs you can't be bothered with or are too busy to do. When you see I'm worth it, then we'll agree a fair price for my time.'

Hare threw back his head and laughed. 'By God, you deserve some help, just for the cheek of you. I have nothing at present I can use you for, but when I do, I will get in touch. But first, tell me what Eric Dyke bought from the second woman he spoke to.'

Bought? I only saw him speak to her, and saw her smile before he walked away.

'You didn't notice, did you? He didn't buy anything, Meg. Eric gave the woman several coins, possibly sent by his father to settle an unpaid bill. If you are to make a good fist of this, then you must see everything. *Everything*. Do you understand?'

'I have to say I'll do my best, sir.'

'Let us hope your best is good enough, Meg. And if we are to work together, my name is Edwin. I have no need of "sir." Leave that to the likes of your master.'

A second later he was gone. I ran down the hill to the river to complete Mr Beaumont's errand, laughing all the way. My pleasure was only in part due to starting a new, and hopefully profitable, career. The other part was that my new teacher didn't know I already noticed many things. Like what I'd seen my mistress do when he walked from Cliffe House after his last visit.

The promise by Mr Hare - by Edwin - gave me so much encouragement I could hardly wait to start and even though he hadn't seemed much impressed with my attempts to follow people, I still thought this the right way to go about it. His words encouraged me to improve. It was one thing to skulk in the shadows behind someone, quite another to do the same in broad daylight.

Edwin had suggested I needed to notice all the detail I saw, and this hadn't occurred to me before. He was right, of course, it'd be important when a culprit was taken before the magistrate. I tried thinking about my first attempts, and my head spun trying to recall all I'd observed. I'd need to talk to Edwin about how he knew which things to note and which to ignore. The same would be true for what I heard. I knew well that people don't always tell the truth, or they say what they think they have seen. Or even just what they believe you want to hear. Did Edwin have a secret for divining who was telling lies, who was storytelling and who was being truthful?

The morning after I'd asked Edwin for his help, my dad sent me to collect some nails to repair a stall gate in the stables. We had a good supply of all except the ones we needed. It was only a short walk to the yard, close by Northgate, and it took only a few minutes for the lad to weigh the nails and enter the cost into my master's account. I'd hoped the trip would provide a decent break from my work, for I wasn't in the mood. I tried to engage him in conversation, but he was surly and seemed as dissatisfied with his lot as I was, so I gave up. With the nails in my bag, I spied Joseph walk past the entrance to the ironmonger's yard. I counted to ten and slipped out to follow him.

It proved fruitless. Nothing interesting came of it. All he did was wander from shop to shop gathering items which Mr or Mrs Beaumont must have requested. Still, it gave me practice, and I was certain he hadn't seen me. I paid particular attention to which shops he went to, who he spoke with inside, and what, as far as I could see, he bought. There was so much to remember I couldn't think how any of it would be of use, but it was what Edwin had told me I should do, so I did.

I watched Joseph all the way into the back of the house. From my hiding place in the shrubbery by the gate I also had an unobstructed view of the front and saw Walter Downes leaving as Joseph went inside.

Downes is my master's cousin, a frequent visitor and, I think, his business partner although, by the look of him, without the magistrate's fortune. He always looks so down at heel. Not so poor as a labouring man, but surely of no great substance. I would have returned to my work, as I should have, if it hadn't been for the way Downes looked about him when he came out of the front door. He even looked down the side, almost as if checking to ensure no-one observed him. Seeming satisfied, he pulled up his coat collar and made his way to the lane by the front gate. I nipped away from the side one, along the wall and dropped in behind him at a respectable distance. He walked straight along High Street, past all the taverns and shops, until he turned into Cartway. Here, waggons, horses, dogs, and people filled the narrow street, moving up towards the town or down to the river, and I found it easier to stay close on Downes' tail with little chance of him seeing me.

The crowd stayed as dense at the bottom, and it was a simple task to keep Downes in sight making his way along the riverbank through Low Town. Once he passed the new bridge, I'd an idea where he might be going and smiled when he entered my master's boatyard, one of three he owned along this stretch of the Severn. By a repair shed, Downes lifted his hat to two men waiting there. I didn't know either, but they both seemed of a similar station to Downes, out of place in this setting. Clearly, neither were my master's workmen. Did Mr Beaumont have customers so shabbily dressed?

The three men spoke for a few minutes, with one pointing one way, and Downes pointing another, before he disappeared inside the shed and brought out two lads. I knew them to be apprentice boatmen, learning the trade and the currents on the river. Downes gave them orders and they left. He returned to his conversation.

I chanced my arm and wandered into their sight, hoping I could hang around nearby and catch what they were saying. Though I knew who Downes was, I didn't think he'd have noticed my presence at his cousin's house, or remembered me if he had, especially in a different place. Just to make sure, I kept my back to the group when I pretended to inspect a craft only ten yards away from them. Even from there, I could only grasp the odd mumbled word, making no sense to me. The lads returned with a barrow carrying several parcels wrapped in sacking.

One of Downes' companions pointed to a horse and cart behind the shed. As he turned back, he noticed me. 'You, girl. What are you doing there?'

I turned, all politeness, innocence, and surprise.

'Me, sir? Nothing, sir. Only looking on the workmanship in this fine trow.'

'Well clear off. It is not a vessel you can afford; I am sure of that.'

If I'd argued, it may have attracted Downe's attention and something may have pricked his memory, perhaps placing me in my master's garden. Good sense said I keep my head bowed, then curtsey and leave.

Walking all the steep way up to home, I was certain I'd uncovered a theft of my master's goods. The problem would be deciding if informing him would be to my advantage. If so, how could I do it without revealing why I'd abandoned my labours to follow his cousin?

Four

Edwin hardly ever drank to excess. He found the muddling of his senses unwelcome, as was the fear he might reveal something of his past to men he would rather not know of it.

Last night had been special. In the latter part of the day, he'd collected a fine bounty from a grateful client, for discovering where his store of gold coins had gone. It turned out the man's wife had taken them to have a good time with her young lover. The cuckold was not pleased but he paid Edwin well for his work. The prize warranted a celebratory drink, though when Edwin had signed the client's ledger for his payment he noticed the date. The anniversary of his father's slaying by red-coated soldiers, and his mother's slaughter after they defiled her. That day he had hidden like a coward. Something he'd vowed he would never do again. That day he had slunk away, taking shelter where he could, searching for men loyal to the King Across the Water. Beginning his first new life. Edwin knew nothing of the Jacobites and what they stood for, only that they were the enemies of King

James, and so allies in his vengeance.

These memories had set the stage, and his celebration had turned into a night of remorse. Friends in The Crown helped relieve Edwin of some of his recent earnings. He matched the drinkers, tankard for tankard, until he collapsed hours later in a corner, the porter and gin a fatal mix. His eyes creaked open as the slap of wet mop on flagstones rattled his brain.

Mercifully, the light was dim, just enough to make out the bulk of the tavern-keeper at his night's end duties. 'Huh. Not dead then, Edwin?'

'Wha?

'Dead. You. Not gone to our Maker? Mind you, not likely, enough spirits drunk to pickle you for a good while.'

The man let out a laugh which hurt Edwin's head so much he gagged. Edwin got to his feet and the room spun. 'What hour is it?'

The tavern-keeper laughed again then spit into his bucket. 'St Leonard's struck two just before you woke.'

'God's truth, I need to go.'

'I expect you have. Mind your brethren on your way out. Can't be having you trip over one and crack your skull on my nice clean floor.'

Edwin had not been the only one overtaken by the liquor. Half a dozen dead-drunk bodies lay on benches or on the ground between him and the door. Outside, in the pitch-black street, Edwin leant against the wall of the drinking den, gulping air to keep the bile from rising in his throat. It worked for only a moment. The next he was bent double, retching. The crisis passed and he scrabbled into his pocket for something to wipe his mouth. Trembling hands curled around a piece of paper, not something he remembered putting there. Even if his evening's drinking had allowed his eyes to focus, it was too dark to read until he groped his way to a lantern still burning outside another alehouse.

The message, short and to the point, in a crude hand, warned him the writer had information that would harm him, that payment was required to keep the secret. It said nothing about how much, when, or how it should be paid, only that the writer would contact him soon.

Edwin stumbled into a corner and puked again.

He'd known the day would come when his life would catch up with him. His allegiances, religious and political, and the blood of an innocent man could not lie hidden forever. He had hoped he would have longer than the three years since he had given up the life of a soldier and moved far away to where no-one knew him. Now, it seemed, it was not to be. Edwin had carved out a new beginning when he settled in Bridgnorth, making new acquaintances, inventing a life story to satisfy their curiosity, and quickly establishing himself as the one to go to when offended against.

His choices were obvious, though none palatable. Find the man, or woman, go on the run again, or let the truth be told.

If he found the person, what would he then do? Kill them? Beat them into submission? If he simply took them to the magistrate, he may as well ignore the threats because his secrets would be exposed anyway. At best he would lose his living, at worst he might find himself imprisoned or transported to a life of slavery.

He could leave the town, try to establish himself again somewhere new, perhaps in London where he might live unnoticed amongst the throng. But Edwin had no desire to leave Shropshire, none at all, not now Sarah Beaumont had crossed his path.

Could he kill someone? He'd killed before, but this would be different. Cold-blooded. And he'd have to work out how to hide what he'd done. Edwin frowned as he considered the possibilities.

All through the night the wind had howled, hail had clattered the windows, and Hannah had fretted with burning cheeks, the child taking no comfort from her mother's ministrations. Aubrey had joined Sarah in her bedchamber seeking comfort of his own but, to his wife's relief, he had retired back to his own room when Hannah's wailing would not stop. After he left, Sarah lifted the child from her cot, drew the curtains around her bed, and cuddled her until Hannah nodded off in the early hours.

When Sarah woke, having slept fitfully, the storm seemed to have raged itself out along with her daughter's discomfort. The girl stirred. Sarah stroked her hair and hoped the crying had been due to the child's last teeth appearing. She lay calmer now at Sarah's side on the bed and looked to be enjoying the attention. Her mother took her hand away for a moment and unfolded the note for the tenth time or more since she had retired. It had appeared the previous day, in the same spot in the garden as the earlier one. There was no name, but an amount of money demanded, and a time and place to deliver it. She had kept it close to her body, believing it would be safe there from discovery by Aubrey. When he had arrived in her room at bedtime, clearly intent on his rights as her husband, Sarah had slid the paper into the bolster cover without him noticing. She had lay like a board, showing no interest in the proceedings, and he had left without satisfaction, slamming the door as he did so.

She had read those last words on the first message, *I will be in touch,* time and again, wondering why the man had not done so. It had been five days, and nothing arrived to say what he wanted. The first hours after she had received it, her mind had been in such turmoil she had given no thought to what she might do. Paralysed by the fear of what would happen if the man revealed her secrets to Aubrey. Later, her mind had become clearer, and she knew she must wait, and fret.

Worry she did. So much so that their visitors had asked on more than one occasion if she was well. If she had cared for either of them, she might have said something. A hint that her head was distracted, that her stomach churned, and she felt she would spew at any moment. But she did not like either Aubrey's friend, or his coarse wife, so she said nothing, other than having a light headache.

Even though Sarah's own background was humble, she could still not imagine how Aubrey would know those people, he was so far above them in station. The woman, Bessy Jenkins, with her pox-marks and common accent, had the vilest tongue on her as Sarah had ever heard. The husband, Josh, was hardly better, and had pulled Sarah to him, slobbering his fat lips over her when he had taken more drink than was good for him. As if this was not bad enough, Aubrey had done nothing to stop the assault, even seeming to revel in her embarrassment.

Three days the couple had stayed, wanting food and entertainment the whole time. This was easy for Aubrey, who had simply taken Josh Jenkins round the taverns, or riding round the countryside to show off his farms and business enterprises. Sarah was forced to take Mrs Jenkins to visit friends, who were clearly as offended as she was by the woman's behaviour. All of the time, thoughts of the note distracted her.

Now, in the quiet of her room, Sarah thought of Edwin Hare. So much more desirable than Aubrey. Tall, handsome, and much closer to her own age. Sarah shook the picture away. This was not what she wanted from him at this time. She would need his skill, and wondered how she might contact the thief-taker without raising her husband's suspicions. In her mind she went through the servants. The options were not good.

Her housemaid, Polly, she would not trust. More than once she had seen Polly flatter Aubrey, probably in the stupid hope he would fall for her, a serving girl, and leave Sarah. True, her husband may have his way with a servant, Sarah was sure of this, but he would not make more of it than scratching an itch.

The cook, Catherine Garris, was loyal to her mistress, but a chatterbox and unlikely to keep a juicy story to herself. The footman, Joseph, his master's man, would probably tell Aubrey to curry favour. Even if he did not, he was not bright and could give her away unwittingly.

Other servants were more distant, and she knew little of them, but Sarah had spied her husband punishing the assistant gardener, Meg, and Edwin Hare's intervention to stop it. The girl would hardly be on Aubrey's side and might be willing to take a message without asking too many questions. It was a risk, but Sarah had little choice.

She put away the message, bent and kissed her daughter on the forehead, then lifted her into her cot. Only when she was sure the child had settled, did she call for her maid to help her dress. Soon afterwards she put on her cloak and left the house.

Freezing gales had blown for two whole days, reaching a peak during the night, scattering leaves and twigs across the garden. By morning, the wind had dropped and changed direction, turning mild. This, with the sun now shining, made me curse the extra layers I'd pulled on when I'd climbed, shivering, out of bed. They only served to make me sweat.

I removed my heavy jerkin and hung it on a branch before returning to gather up the debris. Mr and Mrs Beaumont were no gardeners themselves but demanded we kept the grounds in good order for their enjoyment. Three shovelfuls in, a woman's voice, soft, came from behind me. 'Such arduous work, Meg. Are none of the men around to help?'

I bowed my head and clasped my hands in front, as I'd seen Dad do when addressing his betters. My mistress had never spoken to me directly before, so I prayed I showed enough respect. 'Not today, Madam. My father and the others are away mending fences. Terrible lot of damage they found after the storm.' I stood a little straighter, 'Though this is nothing I can't handle.'

Mrs Beaumont smiled. 'I am sure this is true, Meg. So often we women are underestimated, are we not?'

'I... I'm sure I can't say, Madam. Was there something you wanted of me?'

'Actually, Meg, I wondered if you would be able to do your mistress a favour.'

"Your mistress" not "me". A gentle reminder I'd little choice. 'If I'm able, Madam. What is it?'

She chewed the nail of her middle finger for a moment. 'Before I tell you, are you able to keep a confidence? You must tell no-one.'

I told her I believed myself to be trustworthy but hoped my job would not be threatened by helping her.

'If you keep this to yourself, Meg, there will be no need to worry on that score. Now, I believe you are friendly with Mr Edwin Hare. Is that so?'

'Hardly friendly, Madam. I know who he is, and we spoke when he visited Mr Beaumont.' I saw no reason to tell her of my ambition nor of our more recent conversations.

'But he saved you a beating by my husband?' I said nothing. 'I will take your silence as affirmation. I wish you to take a message to Mr Hare. Will you do this?'

I nodded.

'Tell him I need to talk with him about a most sensitive matter. I will call to his home tomorrow but cannot say what time. It will depend on when I can be free.'

'You know where Mr Hare lives, Madam?'

'Bridgnorth is not a large place, Meg, I will find it. Remember, though, no-one, and I mean no-one, other than Mr Hare himself, must hear of this. You understand?'

I gave her my word that I'd do as she wished. My mistress told me to go as soon as I'd finished my work. If I was asked, I'd to say nothing more than she had sent me on an errand. She left and I returned to my work, wondering why she'd need to speak with Edwin.

It took another hour to collect the leaves and dump them beside the stables, so I could spread them on the vegetable beds when they'd rotted down.

I was grateful for the rest and the walk into town to find Edwin. It took no time to do so, for I saw him walking away from me down High Street, though lacking his usual confident stride, I fell in behind and my tug at his sleeve brought his attention. Edwin turned and scowled, rubbing his forehead. 'Meg?

What is it now? I am most busy today.'

'I've a message for you, from my mistress.'

'From Mrs Beaumont? Then you had best spit it out, my lady, but keep your voice down.' He squeezed the bridge of his nose. 'I am not in the mood for loud noises.

I told him what she'd said, making it as clear he must not reveal her request to anyone. For his part, he pressed me why she wanted to see him. 'I know no more, Edwin, only what I've told you. She couldn't even say what time she'll visit tomorrow, only that she will.'

'Then I suppose I will just need to wait. What are you doing in the town anyway? Following people again?'

I shook my head. 'Not today, sir ... Edwin. I came to find you on Mrs Beaumont's orders and only saw you when I walked on to the street. Are you unwell?'

'Only the result of a little over-imbibing, though my head hurts like it's been kicked by a donkey. You say you've followed no-one *today*? So, you *have* been up to your tricks since I last saw you?'

I couldn't help grinning. 'Once or twice.'

'And what did you see?'

'On the first two times there was nothing of real interest. The footman, Joseph -'

'The one sweet on you.'

'He is no such thing.'

'Do you think I'd miss how he blew you a kiss when I visited the house?'

I felt the blush rise so pinched my side to make it

disappear. 'Well maybe he is, but I have no feelings for him. None at all. As I was saying, Joseph walked into the market, and I followed at a distance. He never saw me once.'

'He is an easy target. But did you learn anything?'

'Nothing, he went on his errands, turned around, and went home again.'

'Then you learned he is a good footman who does his master's bidding. Did he speak to anyone on the way?'

'No-one other than the shopkeepers.'

'Then this confirms what I have said. Who else have you spied upon?'

'Jasper, my master's coachman, but that was only to practise in the dark. He left our room in the evening after we had eaten and did no more than wander round to the Swan tavern. I watched through the window for a while, but he only drank and sang with his friends, so I left him to it.'

'And what did this tell you, Meg?'

'That he likes an ale, and he has a god-awful voice.'

Edwin laughed. 'Well done. Two useful morsels which may come in handy in the future. Is that it?'

I bit my lip, uncertain whether to tell him more.

'Come on, lass, I can see you have something else to get off your chest.'

'My master has a cousin.'

'Walter Downes. I know of him.'

'Two days ago, he left the house, and I trailed behind, keeping out of sight. Not easy because he looked this way and that at every turn, like a man with something to hide. He went down to my master's boatyard.'

'Did he have a bag with him?'

'A bag?'

'On the way there or on the way back? Was he carrying anything to drop off or collecting something to take back?'

'I don't think he did, though I didn't see him return.'

I felt the redness coming again, but Edwin just smiled and clapped his hands. He winced at the sound. 'There you are, Meg, you observed something important, even though you did not know you had. So, what was the purpose of Mr Downes' errand?'

'He met with two men, I did not recognise either, and he ordered a number of parcels to be loaded on to a cart.'

'Interesting. What was in them?'

'I don't know, they were wrapped in sacking. One of the men saw me and chased me away before I could see what was inside.'

Edwin clasped his hands under his chin for a moment, as if thinking. 'Not to worry, this happens sometimes. It certainly looks suspicious though. Something to store in our pockets for another day. I can see we will make a good observer of you, young Meg. Keep practising, and I will give you a real piece of work as soon as I can.'

I could hardly breathe when he gave me this news and coughed to disguise my excitement. I held in the biggest grin of my life until he spoke again.

'And now I must go, Meg, the coroner won't be pleased if I am late.'

'Mr Perry? You have business with him?'

'I work for him from time to time. Occasionally a body might be found which cannot be identified and the coroner will ask for me to discover who might be missing. At other times he may ask me to let relatives know their loved one has died. Usually, though, it will be to investigate the circumstances of a death, in much the same way I would look into a theft. This is what he wants me for today.'

Edwin glanced at the clock above the market hall and held up a palm. 'Now, no more questions. I need to go.'

I wanted to run alongside him, pick his brains about opportunities for work with the coroner, and what the proposed meeting with my mistress might be about. Before I could say another word, he turned and strode away with determination. I guessed he'd not thank me for troubling him further.

Instead, I followed at a distance. I knew where Edwin lived, on St Mary's Street, a lane to the west of the centre of the town, so was surprised when he turned down an alley on the eastern side of High Street. This was also not the route he'd take to the coroner's place of work. I gave him a moment before I went after him. He had told me to practise, after all.

In the blink of an eye, it was clear where he was heading. Though I rarely used it, I knew the alley to come out in the square where lay St Leonard's Church, the opposite side to where Cliffe House stood. The area was quiet at this time of day, with no services and the pupils in their classrooms, so I'd be in real danger of being seen. There was only one thing for it, I'd to hold back, bide my time, and then stroll out boldly, whistling, as if I'd finished my jobs and was heading home. If Edwin saw me, it would look innocent. If he didn't, all well and good.

I needn't have bothered pretending, he wasn't in view. I stopped, leaning against the almshouse's wall. Had he gone into St Leonard's or perhaps one of the Grammar School buildings opposite? Both seemed unlikely. I couldn't chance wandering around the square in case I bumped in to Edwin. Or my master for that matter. Both would want to know why I wasn't back at the house doing my work. Instead, I gave up the task and made my way to the lane which led to the servants' entrance.

As I turned in, I could see Edwin, clear as anything at the side of the front gate, staring up at my mistress's bedroom window. I ducked below the hedge and peeked through a gap. There could be no doubt of what he was doing. He stood stock still, making no attempt to enter the garden, and he even pulled down his hat brim.

It seemed for ever, but I expect it was no longer than two or three minutes before he turned away and walked back towards town. I dashed along the path and dived round the back of the stables where I'd not be seen.

Five minutes later, I was back at my jobs, smiling in anticipation of the adventures which lay ahead.

Five

Sarah Beaumont picked her way through the pigs, hens, and droppings cluttering St Mary's Street, to where Edwin Hare's cottage stood, thankful she had changed into the clothes Aubrey made her wear on their dreary visits to the countryside. The thick, brown, woollen cloak and hood ensured no-one would recognise her. They'd also hide her status. The filth would need to be cleaned from her boots when she got home, but this was a small price to pay for her anonymity. And it was not as though she would get her own hands dirty doing it.

The street was narrow, leading down from the market hall, with a coaching house on one side, though Sarah wondered how anything of a decent size could turn under its arched entrance. Beside it stood some newer houses, tucked between the tumbledown cottages which had been left standing after fire had destroyed much of the town when it was beset by Cromwell's soldiers. She had expected Edwin's home to be finer than it was. Sarah knew the thief taker had as much work as he wanted, and everyone said it paid him well. He hardly lived in a hovel, though this seemed only one step up from the cottages of the carters and boatmen who carry on their trade along the river. A single floor, rough stone walls, and a thatch which had seen better days. Perhaps the man drank or played the dice. She could no longer imagine living in such a place, not since she had married Aubrey.

Her first thought was to wait across the street to see if Edwin came out but realised this might only draw attention, and he might not even be home. Already the children playing in the mud had started to eye her, suspecting a lady who did not belong.

A tap on his door brought him in a moment. 'Mrs Beaumont?'

The fastening of his shirt was not quick enough to hide the purple scar stretching from collarbone to the middle of his chest. Nor to avoid Sarah's blushes. She had noticed previously the intriguing white streak across his jawline, but the one now revealed had been an altogether more serious wound.

Edwin checked each way in the street. 'Your husband is not with you?'

'Not today, Mr Hare. It is I who must speak with you. You received my message?'

'Young Meg passed it on, yes. You had better come inside, away from my neighbours' prying eyes. Come. Quickly.'

The room showed the same lack of care as the outside. A home where a man lives alone and without servants to tidy his mess. Sarah estimated that the whole house would have fitted in her drawing room, and there were no fine carpets or tapestries to lighten its drabness. A thick broth bubbled in a pot hanging from a crane above the fire. Inedible vegetable peelings lay on the table. Edwin swept them up with his hand and threw them on the flames. 'Take a seat, madam. I make no apology for the mess, I do not often receive visitors in the morning, especially any as grand a lady as our magistrate's wife. Now how may I help?'

She sat on a stool, but he remained standing, and made Sarah uncomfortable with the look in his eye. Cruelty? Suspicion? Something else? 'I believe my only option is to be honest with you, sir.'

'Always a good starting point.'

'I have been burgled and need your help to reclaim what was stolen.'

'Mr Beaumont did not mention this when I visited.'

Sarah lowered her eyes. 'That is because he does not know. My husband was away on business, and the items taken belonged to me.' She paused. 'He does not need to be bothered with this.'

'But surely, he would not see it as a bother if his home had been broken into?'

Sarah rose from her seat. 'I have said I do not want him involved. I had hoped you were a man who has discretion and could help me. If I am wrong-headed then I apologise.'

Edwin raised a hand. 'Please stay Mrs Beaumont. It is I who must apologise if I have shown less tact than the situation requires. Tell me what happened, and we will see where it takes us.'

'As I have said, my husband was away for the night. A sound woke me. Thinking of my safety, and that of my child, I stayed in my room ready to defend us if necessary. The man went to my dressing room and took some items. When he had them, he went back downstairs and left.'

'You said "man," could it have been a woman?'

'I am as certain as I can be. The weight on the landing and the gait when they descended the stairs spoke of a man.'

'Then, for now, we will follow that path. You saw them. Did you see his face?'

'I did not.'

'And what was it he took?'

Sarah took a deep breath. 'I cannot tell you.'

'Why not?'

'Because I do not know if I can trust you to keep a confidence. Not yet. Is it not enough for you to understand the items taken are precious to me and I want them back?'

Edwin shook his head. 'I am afraid it is not enough. You have given me no description of the man, so I have no way of finding him. Without knowledge of the stolen goods, I cannot even watch for them being sold on.'

'The thief has no intention of selling them. He is an extortionist.'

'You have received communication from him?'

Sarah passed the messages she had received over to Edwin, who scanned them both twice. 'Have you heard anything further?'

'Not yet, though you see he demands I pay him soon. Are you able to help, Mr Hare?'

It took a minute for Edwin to answer, and Sarah could not decide if it was reluctance, uncertainty, or a lack of understanding of the gravity of her situation. She wanted to tell him the truth but had meant what she had said. She did not trust him enough.

'You must understand, Mrs Beaumont, I am a busy man. To find your thief, with no idea of what he looks like, it would take so much time it would upset my other clients, all of whom are paying me well for my services. Besides, and forgive me if I am wrong, if I were to capture him, he would need to go before the magistrate for punishment, and I take it this would not be of advantage to you?'

'It would not, sir. Please understand I do not seek punishment, only the return of the things he has stolen.'

'Even so, I am afraid on this occasion I cannot help, I would be taking your money under false pretences. I suggest you perhaps pay the villain what he asks and lock your secrets away more securely in future.'

Sarah pressed her fingertips to her closed eyelids for a second, released them, and scowled at Edwin. 'I am disappointed in you, Mr Hare. My husband always speaks well of your work. He says you are a man who will do the right thing, regardless of the cost. I can see he is mistaken.'

She stood, pulled her cloak tight around her shoulders, and left.

Edwin paced the room for a long time after Sarah left. Why had he refused when the woman was so obviously in distress and assisting her would put her in his debt? Perhaps it was the fear of failure. He had told the truth. It would be difficult to find a thief with no distinguishing features other than being a man. Though he had accepted similar jobs in the past. A few coppers dropped here, an arm twisted there, and it was surprising what might be revealed.

His refusal vexed him through the rest of the day and evening, made more pointed by a conversation in The White Horse tavern, where he went to clear his head.

Zeb Garbutt, another thief-taker who mainly worked across the border in Worcestershire, goaded Edwin that he must be losing his touch. 'About to win one of yours, Hare. Pretty young thing too, and worth a good shilling I would wager.'

Edwin shrugged, saying he was not short of work, but the man had continued the game. 'You'd best be careful, I'll soon have all your customers, and you'll have none.'

'Then you must tell me what you are talking about, Garbutt, for your riddles make little sense to me.'

'There is no riddle in it, man, only a fee for me. Lady, well connected I would say, comes to me this very afternoon about a burglary. Precious items stolen. Wants them recovered but kept secret. Said she had spoken to you, and you had rejected the work.'

He grinned with blackened teeth. 'What else could I do but oblige? I left her hanging, though. Not profitable to be too eager, is it? Told her to see me in a day or so.'

Garbutt had few clients and even fewer scruples, so Edwin knew the man would take the money. His reticence a simple trick to raise the price. Whether he would actually do anything to assist Sarah Beaumont was open to question. Although Edwin had kicked back at her husband's suggestion that thief-takers were not to be trusted, he knew the likes of Garbutt did little to enhance their reputation.

Edwin walked away and found a bench in the corner, but Garbutt followed and sat beside him. 'You know, Hare, you're too honest for your own good. There's money to be made in our game, much more if you're willing to take advantage now and again. You and me could clean up if we pooled our efforts.'

Edwin raised an eyebrow. 'How so?'

'Well, take this woman for example. Plenty of money, anyone could see that. Something stolen that she doesn't want anyone to know about. Obvious. Find the goods then squeeze her for every penny she has. Can't go accusing us, can she, else her story would be out. No, she has to pay up and keep quiet. Surprised you didn't think of it yourself.'

Garbutt threw back his head, laughing, and Edwin swung his fist to throw a punch, but his arm was grabbed before he could connect with Garbutt's jaw.

The landlord, Thaddeus Jackson, clutched tight. 'Let it go Edwin. No need to get into a fight with this fool.' Thaddeus glared at Zeb Garbutt. 'And you. Get out. And don't come back if you know what is good for you.'

Garbutt did not move for a long second, glancing firstly at Edwin, then the innkeeper, then the five big men who had moved to stand behind Thaddeus, clearly waiting for instructions. He slid from the bench and skulked away to the door, slamming it behind him as he left.

Thaddeus released Edwin's arm then grabbed him round the shoulder. 'Now, Edwin, I believe you owe me, and these strong fellows, a drink.'

The remainder of the evening was a blur, but Edwin managed to stagger home and fall into bed.

He slept soundly and woke with a thick head, and not a doubt he must warn Sarah against taking up Garbutt's services. The difficulty was, he could not just knock on her door and ask to speak with her. He would need to be circumspect. Half an hour's thinking over his bread and cheese took him to a plan.

I'd been sent by my master to prepare Bella, ready to take him by carriage to visit his tenants by Brockton. The gloomy morning threatened heavy rain, and Mr Beaumont obviously had no desire for a long, wet journey without a shelter over his head. Bella wasn't the prettiest of our horses, but she was placid and sturdy and could pull a carriage all day long over any road or land. If he'd planned a short journey, I'd have groomed one of the others, but this trip would take him a good hour in each direction, part on muddy and rutted tracks, so Bella was the best choice. I'd completed the brushing and was about to fit her bridle.

I almost jumped from my skin when a voice came from the shadows. 'Psst. Meg. Do not jump lass, it is only me, Edwin.'

'God's teeth, sir, what're you doing hiding in there?'

He laughed loud when he stepped into view. 'I am sorry, I did not mean to scare you. I thought you would be made of sterner stuff.'

'I ... I wasn't scared. Just surprised is all. What do you want?' I swung to look outside the stall. 'If the magistrate doesn't have his carriage soon, I will be in for a beating.'

'All I want is a small favour. You can keep another secret?'

I told him I could.

'Then I need to speak to your mistress again without Mr Beaumont finding out.'

'You're out of luck, Edwin, as I've little contact with the lady. As well you know, I work outside and am never in the house, the garden is as close as I might get to her. These chilly days she'd be out there less and less.'

'Ah, but who do you speak to at the door? Your gentleman friend, Joseph, do you not? And he would be able to speak to Mrs Beaumont, I am sure. Just give the footman your finest smile and ask him to pass a message you have been given. Simple.'

Edwin passed me a note, sealed with red wax and

my mistress's name written on the front. Nothing to identify the sender. I turned it over two or three times in my hand, then shook my head. 'I tell you, once again, Edwin, he's not "my gentleman friend", and I'm not so sure I should be helping you to have my mistress betray her marriage.'

'Betray her marriage? Is this what you think I am about, Meg?'

'Well -'

'Stop right there, before you say too much. It is purely business, but business the good lady wants to keep from her husband. If you assist me in this, you will be one step further on the way of learning my craft.'

Before I could protest further, the magistrate yelled across the yard for his carriage, and I had to tell Edwin I'd do as he bid. He reminded me I was to say someone I didn't recognise had approached me in the garden and asked me to pass the note to Mrs Beaumont. I nodded and he slid back into the shadows as quietly as he'd come out.

I waited until Mr Beaumont was away, only a short time later, then knocked at the kitchen door to ask for Joseph. I told him what Edwin had said I should, even topping it off with what I hoped was a shy, though endearing, smile. Joseph didn't appear even remotely suspicious. He grinned, kissed the envelope, though was looking at me, and went inside to take it to our mistress. He hadn't grinned half as much as I did at how well my make-believe had worked.

Six

Sarah looked idly in a shop window, inspecting gloves she had no intention of buying. How much longer could keep up this pretence? St Leonard's bell had rung out for one, the agreed time, minutes earlier. As she turned to walk away, deciding that the meeting with Edwin Hare had been a bad idea, he appeared from St Mary's Street.

He smiled and lifted his hat. 'Good morning, Mrs Beaumont, what a pleasure to bump into you.' The cheeriness in Edwin's loud greeting told the world this was a chance collision of two acquaintances on the street. 'I hope you and your husband are well.'

Sarah picked up the cue. 'Indeed we are, Mr Hare. He is away attending to his business today so I thought I would amuse myself buying some new gloves,' she shook her head and shrugged, 'but none of these are to my liking. I believe I will wander to Mrs Petkin's shop further down.'

'That is the direction I was taking, madam, perhaps you'll permit me to walk with you?' Edwin took a place beside her, far enough to appear respectable, but close enough to be heard without being overheard.

They began to walk, and Sarah lowered her voice. 'You wanted to see me.'

'I'm told you have commissioned Zeb Garbutt to find your stolen items.'

'And what matters that to you, Mr Hare? I asked for your assistance, and you refused.'

'The man is a charlatan, widely known as a thief himself. Garbutt will take your money, and you'll never see him again. If you do, it will be to extort even more from you than the thief would demand.'

'Nonsense. "The man," as you call him, seemed perfectly charming,' Sarah glared for the briefest of moments at Edwin, 'and more willing to help a lady than some I might mention.' Her composed smile returned as a couple approached. She glanced in a window and swept a hand across, indicating the fineness of the display.

As soon as they'd passed, Edwin broke the pretence. 'I never said I was unwilling to help, madam, only that I could not. You provided nothing on which I could work. No description of the thief, no motive, and, worst of all, no detail of what I might be looking for. An impossible task. Does it not strike you as odd that Garbutt says he can find the culprit with so little information? Perhaps you told him more than you told me?'

'Indeed, I did not.'

'Then I can only presume he is either out to cheat you, or he stole the items himself. At least if he did not, one of his cronies did, and Garbutt is willing to give the man up for a few shillings from an easily fooled woman.'

'Or it may simply be he is better at his job than you are, Mr Hare.'

'If that is what you think, Mrs Beaumont, then good luck to you. I'll let you continue with your shopping.'

Edwin turned to walk away. A touch on his elbow stopped him. 'Please do not go, Mr Hare. I am grateful for your concern. Truly. Let us walk and talk some more, and perhaps we may reach an understanding.'

He waited several seconds for his grin to subside before he could turn back to his companion. 'I am sure we will reach that understanding more easily if you tell me everything you know. This might give me some idea where to start the quest to recover your stolen items. Tell me again, for example, in as much detail as you can, the events leading to your loss.'

Sarah nodded, and recounted what happened from the time she woke, to the point where she realised what had been stolen. She explained each step, the checking of her daughter, the creaking floorboards, the sound of opening drawers, watching him through a crack in the door. Even her despairing fall to the ground when the man left the house. Edwin asked if she was sure there was no more.

'There is not. The whole thing was over in minutes. The thief knew what he wanted and where it would be found. I stayed in my room until morning light with the door locked and my back staunch hard against it, fearful he may return. Only when I felt safe did I go through to my dressing room and face the horror awaiting me. He had left no sign of being there, save for one drawer left open, and my precious ... items gone.'

'And you do not feel able to tell me what these *items* are?'

'I do not. What does it matter?'

'It matters because it will tell me where I might look and where I should not bother. Let me explain. If it is gold or jewels, it is a simple burglary, and I would begin by talking to those who deal in such trinkets. Money is a different matter. In such a case I might ask in the taverns if anyone has been spending more freely than usual.'

'There was no money stolen.'

'So, I begin elsewhere, but can we please stop this guessing game, I'm weary of it already.'

Sarah bit her lip, covering it with three fingertips of her right hand, and stared at the ground before returning her gaze to Edwin. 'If I must tell you, then I suppose I must, but you will keep it secret?'

'I assume there would be no point in the whole endeavour if I were to tell all and sundry what it is you have lost.'

'Correct.'

'Then I promise not to say a word to anyone who doesn't need to know.'

'So be it. Amongst other things, there was a precious cloak clasp taken. Gold scrolls and leaves, very finely worked, with flashes of red, blue and green jewels. It was a present from my husband on our betrothal, but this is not my main concern.

'To recount the whole story, I need to go back to my younger days, long before I met Aubrey. I grew up in Ludlow, my father has a cobbler's shop there. When I was fourteen, he took an apprentice. Owen Ambrose was his name, and we became friends.'

'Friends?'

'At first, yes. My father would have it no other way. And so it stayed for a year and a half. Then, one day, Owen told me he was leaving. He had joined King George's navy and would be setting sail within the month. I cried when he gave me the news, for we had become close. That was when Owen kissed me for the first time. Over the next few days we agreed we would write whenever we could and marry when he returned.'

'And these letters were stolen?'

Sarah stopped in her tracks. 'So, you knew all along?'

He shook his head. 'Certainly not, madam, but what else could it be? I am right am I not?'

She began to walk again. 'You are. Owen wrote to me every week, though his news was always delayed as his letters took an age to arrive.'

'I am afraid I do not understand why their loss would be a problem. You were young and unmarried, barely more than a childhood friendship. Hardly something to be ashamed of.'

'At the start, yes. But soon after I became sixteen, Aubrey began to show an interest in me. My father had borrowed money from him to see us through a difficult patch. Aubrey would call each week to collect a payment, then my father fell ill and could not pay.

'Aubrey said he needed a young wife and would forego the debt if I were to marry him. Father resisted, as you might expect, though in the end had to agree. The only concession he could win was that we would not wed for another year.'

'And you continued your correspondence with this Ambrose fellow?'

'Yes. I so wanted to tell him we must stop but I had not the courage. I kept hoping Aubrey would lose interest or become tired of waiting. He did not.

'A week before we were due to marry, Owen returned unexpectedly. He and I had a week where we met secretly every day. Before he left to rejoin his ship, we spent one a blissful night and he had gone when I awoke. He left a gold locket on my pillow. I received another letter after my wedding then they stopped. I was beside myself with worry, partly because of fear of what might have happened to my love ...'

'Partly?'

'And partly because I had discovered I was expecting his child.'

Edwin gasped.

'Do not look so shocked, Mr Hare, I am not engaging you to be my judge. I had been forced into a marriage I did not want, to a man I did not love. I penned a letter to tell Owen of my pregnancy, and to confess I was now married, but before I could send it, I received word Owen had been killed in a battle off Venezuela.' She wiped a tear from her cheek, brushing it away as if a mote had caught in her eye. 'I now had no option but to stay with my new husband and pretend the child was his own.'

'You did not feel you could throw yourself on Aubrey's mercy?'

Sarah laughed. 'You are not serious, sir? You work with my husband almost daily and know the kind of man he is. Generous to those he wishes to impress and ruthless, cruel even, to those he does not. He would have thrown me out on the streets as soon as look at me if he believed I had been unfaithful in the slightest manner.'

'Then why did you not destroy the evidence?'

'I have asked myself the same question a thousand times over the last week. You are correct, I should have. Though I could not bring myself to do it. Those letters and the locket were all I had left of Owen. The trinket and his last one, declaring his undying love, and my final one, returning his love but unsent, were with those stolen. If they fall into Aubrey's hands, he will throw me out,' fear crossed Sarah's face 'and keep my little Hannah.'

The thief-taker stopped and turned to face Sarah. 'You think he would keep your daughter?'

'Without doubt. He sees her as his possession. Even if I confessed she is not his own child, it would not matter. If he could hurt me he would separate us.'

'Then we must get your letters back, mustn't we?'

'You ... you will help me?'

'If it is a choice between you being robbed by that scoundrel Zeb Garbutt and keeping you and your daughter in the comfort you have come to expect, then the choice is a small one. I have clients who can wait a week or two.'

'Then I will be eternally grateful. I will, of course, recompense you for your services.'

'You will indeed, madam, and doubtless you will see your way to put in a good word with Mr Beaumont. A thief-taker is not much in this town without his continued patronage.'

'If you do a good job, sir, you may be sure I will put you in Aubrey's good books.'

She indicated down an alley on their right, and began to speak more loudly, adopting the pose of a lady passing the time of day with an acquaintance she has come upon in the street. 'Here we are, Mr Hare, the shop I want is down here.'

Edwin raised a finger and beckoned her closer once more. 'Before you leave me, madam, have you no idea who may have broken into your home?'

Sarah bit her lip for a moment. 'None at all. One of the house servants may be involved, though I do not think they would have come at dead of night, they would have no need as they could enter my dressing room at most times without remark. It is unlikely to be my husband, is it, as he would not have kept his find secret?'

'Any enemies? Any strangers seen hanging around your gate?'

'Not that I am aware of.'

'Then I will make enquiries where I can. Now, you must go. We are already attracting the noses of our neighbours.'

Sarah adopted the charade again. 'Thank you for your company, sir, I shall be sure to pass on your good wishes to my husband.'

With this, Sarah turned away, making Edwin's tipping of his hat redundant. Nonetheless, he walked on with the barest hint of a self-satisfied smile. He looked forward to passing the news to Garbutt.

Seven

For the last two days I'd struggled to keep my mind on my work, ever since Edwin asked me to deliver his note to my mistress. It wasn't helped by wondering when he'd begin to help me become a thief-taker. Yesterday my master had slapped me round the head again, for the state of his carriage when he'd taken it to Brockton, and my mistress had found me daydreaming in the garden when I should have been weeding around her favourite roses. She is the most pleasant of women but was peevish with me the entire day, picking fault with everything I did.

If I'd my head down, with a clear job to do, then I didn't struggle to concentrate. The problem came when I'd a choice and was undecided what to do next. In these times, my thoughts and my feet would wander to the side of the house, to check if Edwin loitered there waiting for me to appear.

The storms had returned the previous night, with a biting wind from the east taking the last few leaves from the trees, scattering them like feeding swallows swooping in all directions. I wandered over to look at the hedges to see if the wind had caused damage. It was unlikely. They are well protected from the blasts by a property across the lane, and the grammar school walls beyond, but it gave me an excuse to wait close to the gate.

As if he'd read my mind, Edwin appeared from behind one of the elms framing the entrance. He made as if to duck in again then paused and waved when he saw me standing there. It occurred to me he wouldn't have been visible from the house or the garden, though would have a clear view of both from the shadow of the tree. I wondered if he'd been watching for me, or with some other intent.

He tapped a finger to his hat brim. 'Morning, Meg. Glad I've bumped in to you. I was ... just passing and considered calling in to speak to the magistrate. Now I've thought about it, I won't bother him today. Whilst I have you, I need a minute and an ear.'

I looked back at Cliffe House. 'If Mr Beaumont sees me wasting my time again, he won't be pleased, so a minute is all you can have.'

'Let us get on then.' Edwin stroked his chin. 'I need your assistance again.'

At last. My heart skipped a beat. 'In what way?'

'I told you that your mistress has engaged me to deal with a ... er ... delicate matter, didn't I?'

'You did.'

'Well, it seems to me you are well placed to help. Are you up for it?'

For a moment, I hesitated, thinking I shouldn't be involved in the affairs of the house, but I realised such things are the meat and drink of someone making their way as a hunter of criminals and villains. Though, for the life of me, I couldn't imagine how my mistress might be involved in anything so low. 'Tell me what you need, Edwin, and I'll do what I can.'

'Before we go down this path, will you explain something?'

'What?'

When we spoke earlier, you became annoyed when I suggested thief-taking was no trade for a woman. And you said people thought the same of you being a gardener.'

'Of course, I did. How would you feel if I told you that you weren't fit to do a job just because you wear britches?'

'Ha. Good point. So, tell me, how did you become an under-gardener?'

I felt like I'd been punched in the gut. This was not a story I wanted to tell, and held my breath until Edwin prompted me again. 'Meg?'

Now it all spilled out. 'I had a brother, Tim. A year older than me. And he was killed.'

'Killed?'

'Driving a cart for a neighbour. Fell off when it hit a rut and went under the back wheel. Crushed his innards. Tim lasted the afternoon. By the time Dad got back home from Cliffe House he was gone.'

'I'm sorry, Meg. But what ...'

'Tim was the apple of Dad's eye. He brought Tim to Cliffe House when he could and showed him how to do all the jobs. After my brother left us, Dad brought me instead. I've never been sure if it was my help he needed or just the company. When the under-gardener job came up, I know it would have been Tim's if he'd still been alive. By then, though, Dad knew I was able to do it, and pressed Mr Beaumont to take me on.

'But it's not where I want to be forever. I know I can make a good fist of being a thief-taker if you'll just help me. Tell me what you want me to do.'

'First of all, you must swear you can keep a secret. Not a word to anyone, not even Mrs Beaumont herself. Can you do this?'

I snorted. 'Of course. What use would I be as a thief-taker's apprentice if I couldn't keep my mouth shut?'

'Apprentice now, is it?' The frown he'd been wearing turned to a grin which almost split his face in two, 'We'll have to see if you're up to the job yet, my girl.'

One side of my mind told me to reject his insult and walk away, the other side said to stay. Rightly or wrongly, it was the reckless road I chose. I was beginning to understand something of Edwin's nature. Despite his strong exterior he enjoyed a joke, and I'd need to put up with the occasional ridicule if I was to work with him. 'There's no need to make fun, Edwin.'

'You're right, Meg, this is no laughing matter. Something has been stolen from your mistress, and I need you to keep an eye on those in the household.'

'Stolen? What?'

'That I can't tell you, at least not yet. Suffice to say it is of extreme importance to Mrs Beaumont and we must do all we can to find it. Almost two weeks ago a man entered her rooms at dead of night and took something then left. Nothing else was taken, or hardly even disturbed, so he knew what he was looking for. This suggests it was either someone from the house, or who had been guided by someone from the house.' Edwin raised an eyebrow. 'I am safe to assume it wasn't you?'

'If you need to ask the question, Edwin, perhaps I'd better leave you to it.'

'Good girl. Your reply tells me I am right to trust you in this. Now, what you must do is watch for signs. Are any of your workmates free with their money? Do any seem to have a grudge against your mistress? Are they meeting anyone who would normally be outside their circle? This is where all this observing you have been doing will come in useful. Follow them all to your heart's content. But do not arouse their suspicions.'

'So, I'm to follow the servants and report back to you?'

'Not just the servants. The magistrate himself, any visitors, relatives, and so on. Anyone who would know enough about the family to understand where their valuables might be kept.'

'You want me to spy on my master?'

'I cannot imagine he is involved; he would have nothing to gain for he already owns all that his wife possesses, but watch him anyway. He may have an enemy who may wish to harm him by hurting Mrs Beaumont.'

Once again, I'd a dilemma. If the magistrate found me watching him for Edwin's benefit, I'd be out on my ear, and him so influential in the town I'd not find another employer. But, if my mistress was indeed in danger, as Edwin suggested, my master wouldn't be happy if I did nothing to help keep her safe.

I had no alternative but to agree to Edwin's wishes. I could only pray the skills I'd been working on would keep me free from discovery. 'You know I can do as you ask, but I'm not happy with it. Mr Beaumont is a powerful man, and he'll throw me on the dung-heap if he finds what I've done. My mother needs every farthing I can spare, so if he discovers I've played a part in this you must promise to explain I was only doing your bidding to help my mistress.'

Edwin lifted a hand and placed it on my shoulder. 'You are a good and faithful servant to them both, Meg. Worry not, I will do all in my power to protect you, though there is one condition.'

'Which is?'

He burst out laughing. 'You must do all in *your* power not to make a sow's ear of the job.'

I supposed I must get used to his jokes and it was no worse than what some of the other servants would say to rile me.

Robins and blackbirds tugged at worms exposed by my father's turning of a vegetable plot. They stuck to their feeding when I dumped the latest barrow of manure on the steaming pile. He only had two rows to finish and would then spread the muck, adding goodness for the next crop.

He didn't stop when I spoke to him. 'Dad?'

'What is it, Meg?'

'Can I ask you a question?'

'It seems like you already have.'

He always has a way with him of making light when he sees I've a concern, smoothing the path to an easy talk. We mostly talk easily anyway. My mother isn't able to live with us, so he and I have been close since my brother was taken from us. But I know he makes an extra special effort when it's needed.

'No, this is a proper question. What would you do if someone asked you to do something which might harm you, but would help someone else?'

'A lot of somethings and someones in there, girl, all a bit vague for an old blockhead like me. Can you tell me more?'

'Not too much. It concerns our master and our mistress.'

My father finally paused in his digging, rested his foot on the blade of his spade, and clicked his tongue. 'That would be a difficult one, I would say. If I thought either of them was in trouble, I'd not hesitate to put myself in harm's way to save them. Her more than him though, I must admit. But I am me and you are you. You must do what you think is best. How might you be harmed?'

'I could lose my job.'

'Then it *is* serious, and I'm guessing it's Mrs Beaumont who needs the help and the magistrate himself who might be taking it out on you?'

'I can't say, Dad. It's best if we leave it there, you've answered my question, and I'm grateful for it.' I turned the barrow around. 'You seem to have enough muck, so I'll put this back in the stables, then I've errands to run.'

I didn't allow him time to come back to me but walked on down the path. I believe he understood because I was barely ten steps away when the rhythm of his steady turning of the soil began again. With the barrow stored, and my hands washed, I set off into town.

At the far end, the market echoed with shouts, the traders attempting to attract buyers for their wares. There's a market several times a week in the town, but today, Wednesday, and on Saturdays, it's much bigger, spilling from the shelter of the space beneath the town hall and along the street. Competition is fiercer and prices a bit lower when it's like this, so I soon collected the few things I needed and was about to return home when I spied Joseph. I decided to follow him again, hoping it would produce more than the last time.

I leant against a wall for a minute, and when he turned away from the market place, I guessed the chase would become more fun. Keeping a good distance, I watched Joseph take a road on the right leading down towards the river. It is known as the Cartway. The houses in this part of the town are little more than hovels, with the vilest of rubbish stinking outside, pawed over by dogs and snotty children. Whilst he walked, Joseph looked this way and that until, halfway down the hill, he reached an alehouse, The Antelope, where a small, thin, man leant against the wall. A scarf covered his face, and Joseph looked shocked when this man briefly pulled it aside. They spoke a few words, and the man held out his hand. Joseph dropped a few shiny coins in it. The footman held out his own hand, but the man shook his head and grinned, then Joseph pushed him. I thought a fight would begin, but something was said and Joseph stopped in his tracks, shook a final fist, and stormed back in my direction. It was all I could do to dive out of sight before he saw me. From my hiding place, I watched the man scuttle across the street and dive down an alleyway between two cottages.

In the time I waited for Joseph to pass, it gave me chance to run through what I'd witnessed. Apart from the argument and the exchange of money, I realised though Joseph had recognised the person he'd met, he hadn't expected to. This, surely, would be useful to Edwin.

All afternoon I wondered what had been going on between Joseph and the man he met on Cartway. They'd neither met as friends, nor parted as friends, of that I was sure, though I was equally certain they knew each other. So, what connection did they have? Why had Joseph handed over money? And what had he expected to receive in return?

I couldn't knock on the kitchen door of Cliffe House and demand an answer from the footman. He'd just slam it in my face. What's more, if my master or mistress heard us, we'd both be in serious trouble. Something I didn't seek nor need; I'd been in the bad books enough over recent weeks. I'd no option but to wait for my chance to come.

The clock in St Leonard's had just struck the half after eight o'clock when I spied Joseph slip from the house. The sun had been down well over an hour. Mr and Mrs Beaumont would have finished their evening meal, and Joseph's duties were completed for the day. He would be escaping to the tavern as was his nightly habit. I knew him to work hard, and never seen him the worse for drink, so the magistrate gave him leeway to relax at day's end. I tiptoed quickly down the stairs from my loft, taking care not to attract attention from any of the other outside servants, then dashed across the grass to head off the footman in the side lane.

I only got there a minute before him but there was plenty of foliage for me to quickly slide behind. My lair was hidden in shadows thrown by the three-quarter moon. The gate creaked, and I heard his steps on gravel as he approached. I swear I'd have died if someone did to me what I did to him.

The poor man leapt back when I jumped from the shadows. 'Sweet Jesus!' He recovered quickly, planted his feet, and raised his fists. 'Hold there, I'll give you more than you bargained for.'

'Calm, Joseph, calm. It's only me, Meg.'

'God's teeth, girl, what are you doing out here at this time?'

'I could ask the same of you, what's sauce for the gander is sauce for the goose. Anyway, I need to talk to you.'

'About what?'

'About things I saw today. On Cartway.'

Joseph lowered his hands to his side and frowned, taking a moment or two before replying. When he did, it was with a house-servant's shrewdness in his eyes. 'And what "things" would these be to be bothering an under-gardener?'

'Coins changing hands and an argument.'

'You saw?'

'I said I did.'

'What business had you down there today? It's not somewhere I'd expect you to be.'

I daren't tell him I'd been following him, on the instructions of Edwin Hare. I could have pretended Mr Beaumont had sent me on an errand to his boatyard, but Joseph could easily have asked our master about this in a casual way. It seemed easier to sidestep his question. 'That's not important, Joseph. What is, is that I saw you. So, what that about?'

He shook his head. 'I can't tell you.'

'It had something to do with Mrs Beaumont though?'

He stepped back as though I'd pushed him. 'How ... how can you know that?'

'It was a guess, a simple one, and you've just told me I'm right.'

Joseph turned away, shaking his head, and made to stride back towards the house. 'No, no, this cannot be. I promised my mistress it would be a secret between us. I have betrayed her trust.'

I grabbed him by the arm. 'Wait, Joseph. You've done no harm, it's not your fault you were seen, and I promise you this. I'd do nothing to hurt Mrs Beaumont.

The footman stopped and looked me directly in the eyes. 'You promise?'

'Of course. Why would I wish to harm her? She's gentle and mostly been good to me. Now, come on, I'll walk with you into town, where you can buy me an ale and tell me what you've been up to.'

Joseph fell in beside me when I started on my way, and I hoped he wouldn't see this as some kind of beginning of a tryst. He kept quiet, so I couldn't tell what he was thinking, though he kept a respectful distance between us. I didn't find him unattractive, but I had higher thoughts of a suitor than a mere servant. Regardless of this, the darkness of the night and the quietness of the streets forced me closer by his side before long, and it was with some relief when we came at last to the Pig and Castle with an open door and a warming fire. There were few customers, and this is perhaps why Joseph had steered us past his usual drinking hole of the Swan. There, he would be well known and teased for being accompanied by a young woman.

He pointed me to a corner and called the landlord for two jugs of beer. Even when we had these in our hands, Joseph was still tight-lipped.

After a minute, I pushed him. 'So?'

'What?'

'Come on, Joseph, you know you're going to have to tell me what was going on down in Cartway. Who was the man you rowed with?'

He drew a deep breath. 'He was a drinking companion.'

'Here?'

'No, in Swancote, where my mother and father live. I have not seen him in a dog's age, not since I came to Bridgnorth. I didn't recognise him until he spoke.'

'Then why did you argue?'

'The man is a rogue, and I fell out with him at home through his bad ways and dishonesty. I didn't know he was living in the town, but even if I had, I wouldn't have sought him out. This morning our mistress gave me a place where a man would be waiting and some money to take to him, I have no clue why. He was to pass me something to return to her. When I handed over the cash, he refused to give back the items, laughing and saying if I stole more for him, he would make it worth my while. I told him in no uncertain terms I was not his lackey and was faithful to my employers, so would do nothing for him.'

'So, what did Mrs Beaumont say when you told her?'

'She said very little, though appeared close to tears. As I was myself if I'm honest, for letting her down. I apologised as strongly as I knew how, and she told me it was not my fault, so to forget all about it. I have not forgotten, though I am unsure what else I can do.'

I leant back and looked him up and down. 'You're young, Joseph, and strong. Why didn't you fight him to get back what he was holding from you?'

'Because it would have served nothing. He is a wily creature and would almost certainly have hidden the material. I don't know what I would have been looking for, so the task would be impossible. When I returned, our mistress didn't seem to be of a mind to say what it was.'

I was about to ask Joseph his old companion's name when a tall, unkempt, lad joined us and threw an arm around the footman's shoulder. His words were slurred by the drink he'd clearly enjoyed for the evening. 'Joseph, Joseph, my friend. What're you doing in here,' he leered across at me, 'with this handsome girl?'

Joseph blushed almost as much as me, and said we worked together, that was all, and we'd bumped into each other a few minutes earlier. He stood, wrapped his own arm around his friend's waist and the two walked off, laughing. Joseph glanced over his shoulder at me as they did, raised his eyes to the ceiling and gave the slightest shake of his head. His lips mouthed 'I will talk to you later' before he turned back and shouted for more beer.

Soon after this, I left the alehouse. The wind lifted and rain began to fall until I was in sight of Cliffe House, when the cloud broke to let the moon shine through again. I stopped for a moment to take in the damp branches glistening in the eerie white light.

If the evening had stayed as murky as only minutes earlier, or if I'd come round the corner minutes later, I may not have seen Mr Beaumont leaving the house. He wore dark clothes in all weathers. With his cloak wrapped round, and his hat pulled down to keep out the chill, he'd have been invisible on a rainy night. I watched until he was half way to the front, then I pulled down my own hat again and dashed along the lane. Being as quiet as I could, I edged behind a tree and watched until the magistrate emerged from the gate. This was going to be amusing.

I stayed a decent distance away, keeping to the blackness by the hedges and walls where even the moonlight didn't penetrate. Bridgnorth houses no more than two thousand souls, even when High Town, where I live, and Low Town, down by the river, are taken together. It would take less than one quarter of an hour to walk from one end to the next in any direction, save for climbing the steep hill if travelling East to West. Beyond the limits of the town there are only open fields, and I was certain my master would have ridden if a farm or village had been his destination. It seemed to me unlikely he would just be out for a stroll at this time of night, and the purpose in his step suggested he'd somewhere in mind.

I needed to be more careful when we reached High Street, for it was lighter here, with lanterns hanging from houses and shops. Mr Beaumont went down a lane in the direction of St Mary Magdalene's. Surely, he couldn't be going there? As a man of standing in the town he must follow his religious obligations, but

I'd never thought him to be devout. Not in a way which would take him to church when not a holy day, especially at this time of night. In any case, if prayer was what he was after, why not just cross the lane from Cliffe House and go into St Leonard's?

When I turned the corner, he was nowhere to be seen, though he'd not been far enough ahead to have reached the church in that time. The mystery was solved by loud laughter pouring from a tavern part way along.

A fellow about my own age, stumbled drunk from the doorway, showing why people were laughing. It gave me a way in without attracting too much attention. I bent, grabbed both his hands, and hauled him to his feet. 'Jack,' a fair stab at his name I thought, 'let's get you back inside. I'll let you buy me a drink, even if you've already had your fair share.'

My new friend shook his head and peered through bleary eyes, grasping for recognition. 'Jack? Why're you callin' me Jack? Nat's me name.'

Not that good a stab after all. 'Course it is. Nat,' I gave him my best smile, 'how could I forget?'

I tugged down my hat, hooked my shoulder under my new friend's armpit, and lifted him over the threshold. 'C'mon, Nat, let's have some fun.'

The Drovers Arms had two rooms on the bottom floor, a long narrow one at the front, stuffed with labouring men and women of all classes. Market traders, seamstresses, builders, and boatmen, all seemed to be in the same state as Nat. Some laughing loud at their companions' silly jokes, others slumped on barrelheads, tankards half-full and untouched since they'd settled there, the Lord knows when.

Beyond this scene from hell, lay another room, only slightly less chaotic, but smaller numbers. The wigs and fine clothes of the men in there set them aside from the low folk where I stood. I spotted my master, the odd one out, bare-headed, in a corner, and a woman on his knee. A bawd without doubt. Not as refined, nor as pretty, as my mistress by a good mile.

I relieved Nat of enough of his cash to buy the pair of us a drink, then sat, watching, over his shoulder, hoping my master would be too preoccupied with his catch to notice me. After a while, he whispered in her ear. She giggled and pulled him, with no resistance that I could see, up the stairs to the floor above. A place I daren't follow, even if I'd wanted to.

My only thought when I left the noise of the tavern behind was how much of this story I should pass on to Edwin, and how much to keep to myself.

Eight

Edwin leant in towards Sarah to speak. This pretence of meeting by accident was becoming tedious. Edwin, at least, would have preferred the warmth and comfort of a coffee house for their meetings, but this would be socially unforgivable for ones with their difference in class and sex. At least for the time being. For now, they would have to settle for seemingly chance encounters on the street.

'Have you heard anything further of your stolen items, Mrs Beaumont?'

Sarah gave a sharp shake of her head. 'Nothing since the second message, which said to send money, and my letters would be returned.'

'When will you do this?'

'It is done already. I sent our footman.'

'So, you have them back?'

'No, I do not. The man refused to give them to Joseph and demanded more.'

'Then at least you know who the thief is. Tell me and I will approach him on your behalf. I am sure we can reach a settlement,' Edwin grinned 'without it hurting him too much.'

'Joseph wouldn't say. He seemed so frightened by the episode; I had to tell him everything was in order and he need not worry himself.'

'Then I will need to ask Joseph about it as soon as I am able to be discrete. In the meantime, I have been thinking about your liaison with Owen Ambrose.'

'Oh?'

'Can you think of anyone who may have known about it. Apart from your parents, of course.'

'The same thing has been occupying my mind. As I told you, all of that happened when I lived in Ludlow. Only two of my friends knew Owen was any more to me than my father's apprentice, and I would trust them both to be discreet. Aubrey has always wished me to put away my life before I met him, so I have seen neither during my time in Bridgnorth.'

'So, there's no-one?'

'Not quite. Owen had a friend, of the name of Matthew Kemp who he'd known since childhood, and we were introduced.'

'Could it have been him?'

'I doubt it. Matthew seemed a most decent man, and I cannot imagine he would be involved in anything like this.'

'So why do you mention him?'

'Because Owen would have told him about us and … I believe I saw him in Bridgnorth only a week before my letters were stolen.' Sarah stopped and examined a shop window, before continuing. 'I had been to church on Sunday morning and was returning when I spotted a man across the green. He appeared to be staring towards our house. As I drew closer, I had a good view of his face. If it was not Matthew, then it was his double.'

'Did you speak to him?'

'I did not. If I had, and been seen by my husband, there would be questions to answer. Questions I would not wish to answer. The man glanced in my direction and held my gaze for a moment, but with no flicker of recognition. He then walked off, not in any kind of a hurry, just as if he had been out for a stroll and was now continuing on his way. This made me wonder if I had been mistaken.'

A light drizzle started to fall, and Edwin stepped aside whilst Sarah put up her umbrella. A moment of awkwardness followed because he was so much taller than Sarah that the spokes kept him at a distance, and if he had ducked under the umbrella's cover he would have been so close to her it would appear unseemly. He did not speak again until sure they were out of earshot of passers-by. 'And you have not seen him again?'

'No, though I have kept my eyes open for him. I would approach Matthew as long as it was not somewhere my husband might see us. He was a good friend of Owen, and I'm sure he would have grieved as much as I when he was killed. It would be nice to talk to him about it.'

'Then I will need to look for him. Describe Kemp as well as you can, and I will begin to ask questions about the town. If I cannot find him in Bridgnorth, then I shall look further afield. But remember one thing.'

'What?'

'You have not seen this man for some time, and circumstances may have changed for him. It is not beyond the bounds of possibility that even if he did not commit the act himself, he could have passed information to the thief. Your Mr Kemp may have done it willingly or unwittingly, but he could still be at the heart of it, and I will find out.'

Edwin had little trouble discovering where Matthew Kemp was staying. Most of the inns and taverns in the town had rooms which were let to working men and women for a few pennies a night, but they were rough places with no furnishings other than a straw bed on the floor. They would be unlikely to attract a traveller who might afford something better. Edwin considered Matthew Kemp would fall into this category, so concentrated his efforts on visiting the coaching inns. He was in luck at the second one he tried, the Pig and Castle, on the High Street, not more than two or three minutes' walk from Sarah's home.

A quiet word with the innkeeper, where a drink was bought and money changed hands, provided Edwin with the information that Kemp had arrived from Ludlow two weeks earlier. Allegedly he had business to attend to. The man still occupied a room at the back of the hostelry, though was due to leave next day. Edwin agreed to return in the evening when Kemp would be pointed out to him.

Edwin returned soon after six o'clock and took up a place where he had full view of the door. A few other men occupied tables, some taking a meal, others reading broadsheets or what appeared to be business papers. The innkeeper had shaken his head when Edwin came in, indicating Kemp had not yet arrived.

Not more than ten minutes later, a man came in and took a seat in the centre of the room. He was short, at least compared to Edwin, and thin. His hairpiece and clothes suggested a man of commerce, though not a rich one. Perhaps a shopkeeper or a trader of some sort. His tanned face spoke of someone who spent much time outdoors, so more likely the latter.

The innkeeper brought him a flagon of ale and placed it on the table. He glanced briefly in Edwin's direction and nodded, then back to his customer. 'Good evening, Mr Kemp, have you had a profitable day?'

'I have, sir, at least enough to have made my visit worthwhile.'

'I'm pleased to hear it. Now, will you be eating this evening? We have an excellent stew.'

Kemp nodded and the innkeeper left to prepare his meal. Edwin approached and indicated the spare chair. 'May I join you, Mr Kemp?'

Matthew Kemp peered at Edwin, as if seeking to recognise him. Kemp placed his hands on the chair arms and half-lifted himself. 'Do I know you, sir? I am sorry, your face is not familiar.'

'I do not believe you do, though I know of you. I

also believe we have an acquaintance in common, a lady of the town.'

Kemp's eyes narrowed. 'I am not of Bridgnorth, sir, and know very few in it, who is the lady to whom you refer?'

'A Mrs Sarah Beaumont, you knew her before she married. '

'Sarah? The one who lived in Ludlow?'

'That would be her. You know she lives here?'

'I do.'

'And you were spying on her home three weeks ago.' There was no question in Edwin's words.

'I was not spying, as you put it. This is only the second time I have been to Bridgnorth, and both times within a month. Before I came the first time, I mentioned to her father I intended to visit the town on business. He told me she now lived here with her husband, the magistrate, and gave me his name. It was easy to find the house and I stood on the corner once or twice, hoping I might contact an old friend.'

'If this is the case, Mr Kemp, why would you not simply knock at the door and make your introductions?'

'Your interest in the subject suggests you may already know the answer to that question, so I will not beat about the bush. My acquaintance with the lady, as you have said, was before she married, and when her affections lay elsewhere than with the man who later became her husband. It would not be right for this to have been mentioned in Mr Beaumont's company.'

'Then why did you hurry away when she spotted you across the green?'

'She saw me? I did not know. If I had, then I would have approached her. It is some time since we last met and I am sure she is much changed.'

Edwin considered his next words carefully. He often used prior knowledge or a direct accusation to shock someone into revealing more than they intended, or even into an admission of guilt. This man did not seem the type to be shocked easily. No, a different tactic would be required. 'Tell me, Mr Kemp, about how you know Mrs Beaumont. I already have some of the story from her lips, as you have surmised, but I would like to hear it from you.'

Before Kemp could reply, his meal arrived. Edwin asked the innkeeper to bring him the same and two more drinks.

Kemp waited until their host moved away. 'I did not know Sarah until I was introduced to her by my friend, Owen Ambrose, even though we were both brought up in the same town. He and I had become friends at school there, and stayed close when we started work, he as an apprentice to Sarah's father, and I as clerk to a dealer in fine fabrics. For my part, I progressed well, and my employer soon raised me to a level where I could represent him in his dealings with suppliers. Mostly this was in the wool trade, but he also buys and sells other cloths, including cotton. This business took me away often, so Owen and I did not see each other much for a while. On one such trip I was away when Owen was killed, though I did not know of it at the time. I had been sent to the West Indies to oversee the establishment of a plantation. My employer had purchased it to have his own supply of raw materials, rather than relying on the vagaries of the market place.'

'So how long were you away?'

Kemp stroked his chin. 'I left about the same time Owen sailed on his first voyage, and I returned home to Ludlow only three months ago. When I did, I called to visit my old friend's family, and only then did I discover he had been killed in action. My first thought was to call on Miss Norris ... I apologise, Mrs Beaumont ... but my father informed me she had married.'

'And you waited a full three months to look for her?'

Kemp pushed away his plate and took a swig of ale, banging his mug on the table when he'd finished. 'Listen here, Mr Hare, I have no reason, nor desire, to be questioned by you in this way. I have only talked with you this far because you claim to have the interests of the lady at heart. Had you not, I would have been tempted to invite you outside for a thrashing.'

Edwin grinned. 'I would wish you good luck with that, Mr Kemp, but let's not quarrel. I *am* acting in Mrs Beaumont's best interests and if you answer truthfully you will have nothing to fear from me.'

Matthew Kemp remained quiet; his lips tight like a scolded child's.

Edwin had questioned enough men to know when

to remain silent and to let them stew in their own thoughts. It took only a couple of minutes before the pressure loosened Kemp's tongue once more. 'To be honest, after my initial concern, I could not think what I would say to her. Owen had gone, never to return, and she had transferred her attentions to another. What would be served by my meeting with the lady?'

'But you changed your mind.'

'Only because I had to come to Bridgnorth to visit an important client of my employer, Mr Barnabus Child of Ludlow. Even so, I spent the whole of my journey and the first day here, wrestling with a decision whether to search her out, or not. Eventually, I decided I would, so wandered round there and was considering how I might approach her if she came out from her home. I stood on the green for a half an hour with no sign of Mrs Beaumont, then I needed to leave for an appointment. I cannot believe I missed her by just a few seconds. It seems if I had done the pious thing and gone into church, I may have been rewarded by seeing Sarah.

'Then I could have made an approach and asked her to meet me somewhere more discrete. I imagined that if she agreed, she would wish to talk about Owen, as I do. If she did not agree, or failed to turn up, it would be obvious she had indeed moved on, perhaps to better things, and would welcome no threats from her old life.'

'Threats?'

'Only in the sense that she may not wish her

husband to be aware of any past ... how shall I put it ... friendships.'

Edwin leant forward, resting his elbows on the table and his chin on intertwined fingers. 'And there you have it, Mr Kemp. Our magistrate's wife is a prime target for extortion. You know of her secret, and you appear after several years only when proof of her relationship with your friend has been stolen. I believe you can see why I may need to talk to you.'

Kemp shook his head. 'If you think I would have anything to do with such a scheme then you know nothing of me.'

'That is true, Mr Kemp, I *do* know nothing of you.'

'Then speak to my employer and he will tell you I have no need of money. I am not a rich man, but I am not poor either. Living in the West Indies is cheap, and I saved, and invested, most of my earnings whilst I was away. I doubt any sum I might extract from Mrs Beaumont would match what I have accumulated, and it certainly would not compensate for how badly I would feel if I caused her harm. I like to think of myself as an honest man, Mr Hare, and I am hurt you do not see me the same way.'

'I hope you will understand, sir, this is not a personal thing, I merely try to get to the bottom of what has happened. If you can provide me with where you were on Sunday night and Monday morning, two weeks past, it is at least one step towards showing you are not involved.'

'One step? I am not sure I understand.'

Edwin breathed deeply and leant back in his chair.

Sometimes he tired of these games, cajoling stories from people. Often, they were lies. It would be quicker to shake the truth from them, but this only worked on the lower orders of men. Characters like Kemp needed more careful handling. 'I am sure you will recognise, Mr Kemp, that it would be possible for two rogues to be engaged in an enterprise such as the one I am looking into. One might carry out a robbery, the other might oversee the whole affair, providing information and finances as might be required. Keeping his hands clean you might say. I simply meant that whilst I may be able to discount you from the one if you could show you were somewhere else, I could not necessarily discount you from the other. Now, please provide me with what I ask, and we can take it forward from there.

'On the night you mention, I would have been in Leominster. My employer recently invested in a watermill there which has been converted to use new machinery which weaves cotton, much reducing the need for skilled workers. I rode over on Sunday afternoon and was there all that week ensuring the quality of the fabric produced from the fibres we ship over from the plantation.'

'Can anyone vouch for this, Mr Kemp?'

'Mr Child will confirm he sent me there. The manager of the mill, a Mr Musgrave, gave me board whist I was in the town, and I dined with him and his family every evening. If you were to write to him, I am sure he will also confirm my whereabouts.'

Edwin made a quick calculation and deduced it would take a minimum of six or seven hours to ride from Leominster to Bridgnorth and back again, including time to rest his horse. So, it would be just possible for Kemp to leave his hosts, pretend to go to bed, allow the household to settle, and then make the journey to steal Sarah Beaumont's letters, returning before they rose again.

Edwin put this to Kemp, who shrugged. 'I have to admit, Mr Hare, I could have done as you suggest, but I did not, and I sense even you do not think it likely. However, you must take such steps as you think fit to prove or disprove my story.'

'In that case I will contact your Mr Musgrave and if he replies favourably as to your whereabouts and your character then we may put this matter to rest. Once this is done, I can ask Mrs Beaumont if she will meet with you, if this is something you still desire.'

'Then I am in no doubt my name will be cleared. I would be eternally grateful if you could speak to her on my behalf. If she does not wish to meet, then so be it.'

Nine

Edwin had not slept well since he had found the cryptic message in his pocket the previous week. He ran over and over in his mind how he would best deal with the situation when he was next approached. He had no doubt that he would be approached. Between evening meal and bedtime each evening, by light of a candle, he read the words until they were fixed in his brain.

I know about you. All your secrets. The blood on your hands. It will cost you, one way or the other. I will be in touch.

The message suggested his tormentor knew a lot, but exactly how much? What might it take to silence him?

Even when Edwin dismissed these thoughts from his head, his sleep was tortured with dreams of flight and bloodshed. His mother and his father, apart but bonded together in their savage death. A priest with a friendly face, making the sign of the cross whilst broken and hacked bodies lay in all directions. Redcoats and blue saltires, all stained crimson. A castle wall, and the face of the last man he had killed.

The morning after he had spoken with Matthew Kemp, Edwin rose late, following a particularly tortured night. He ate with little enthusiasm before penning a letter to Kemp's employer asking him to confirm his man's story. As he wrote, Edwin knew it to be a waste of time. Kemp wouldn't tell a tale which could be so easily disproved. It would need more digging than this. Even if Barnabus Child *had* sent him to Leominster, it did not mean he was with the mill-owner, Musgrave, when he said he was. He could also have been in league with the thief, or given away the existence of the letters by accident.

Since becoming a thief-taker, Edwin had made it his business to become acquainted with the pedlars who set up shop on Bridgnorth's market. Some lived in the town, others were itinerant, buying their wares cheaply in one place then selling them for a profit in another. Both were valuable sources of information because between them they knew everyone coming to the market, and everyone working on it. If stolen goods came up for sale, it would be only minutes before the word was around. Likewise, if Edwin was looking for someone, he could ask any of these traders and if the person was seen in any market within twenty-five miles Edwin would be contacted. It was to the travelling pedlars he wished to speak.

After approaching three, Edwin found one who would be leaving later in the day for Ludlow, and it was to him he entrusted the letter. 'Take this to Mr Barnabus Child ... you know him?'

The pedlar confirmed he knew Mr Child's premises well, having purchased bolt ends of fabric from him occasionally.

'Then, as I say, take this letter and give it to him at your earliest opportunity.'

'You would not put it with the post boy, sir?'

'I could, but I would trust you more than one of those scoundrels who would throw it in a ditch if they thought they could get away with it. You, I expect, will be back here, and you have more to lose than them if you do not deliver it. Take an answer, a simple "yes" or "no" will suffice, and pass it to someone coming back this way.'

The man took the message and stuffed it in the pocket of his jerkin, and the coppers which Edwin gave him into a purse hanging from his belt. He promised he would make the delivery by noon of the next day.

As Edwin turned to leave, he spotted a boy watching him from about ten feet away. Edwin knew him to be Will Trusk, the son of the keeper of the Brown Bell inn. He waved the boy over. 'Here, Will. You wanted something?'

'A man has sent me, sir. With a message.'

The lad shuffled his feet and bit his lip.

'Spit it out then. I have not all day to waste.'

'There is someone who wishes to meet with you. Says it will be to your advantage.'

'And who is this man?'

'I don't know his name, sir, and his face was covered. He collared me outside my father's inn and asked if I knew you. I said I did, so he told me I must find you and give you his message.'

'So where am I to meet him?'

'He said you should be by the gate of Saint Mary Magdalene's church at the time of vespers this evening. You are to go alone, and he will approach you when he is sure it is safe.'

Ten

From across the market place, I watched Edwin. I'd spotted him when I was returning from my tasks at St Mary Magdalene's churchyard. I hadn't seen him for two days and wanted to tell him what I'd discovered, but thought I'd stand back for a few minutes and see what he was doing. He spoke firstly to a man I didn't know, a pedlar by the look of him, then a boy who I recognised to be from the Brown Bell, one of the rougher taverns of the town. Edwin looked like he'd asked a favour of the man, with the two nodding then shaking hands. After he spoke to young Will he looked troubled.

The boy ran off in the direction of his home and I strode out from my hiding place, waving to Edwin and weaving through the market, as though I'd only just seen him. The flicker of a smile which crossed his face quickly returned to the frown he'd been wearing when he didn't know I was looking.

'Morning, Edwin. What's the problem? Your face is dark as thunder.'

'It is nothing to worry you, Meg, simply a little inconvenience I could do without.'

'Can I help?'

'As a matter of fact, you might. If you are able to get away this evening? It should take no longer than thirty minutes.'

I said that I could unless my master or mistress needed me.

'Then I want you to go to the church at the far end of town later, where you were tending the grounds.'

'Saint Mary Magdalene? I have just returned from there.'

'Then I would like you to go back in a few hours. Take up station a little before six o'clock. Somewhere you can see the gate but not be noticed. Perhaps if you pretend to be tidying around the church entrance as the congregation arrives for vespers, you will not look out of place. Can you do that?'

'I don't see why not. If Mr Beaumont asks where I've been I'll have many witnesses to testify I was doing his good works.'

'Good. When you are in position, watch for the man who approaches me. If he shows his face, which I doubt he will, see if you recognise him. If he does not, then follow him when he leaves. Keep a good distance, mind, but stay with him until you find where he is living, then come round to my home, without delay, and tell me. You understand?'

'Of course. Are you going to tell me why?'

'Do I need to?'

'Not this time. But I'll not be at your beck and call

like a servant. We agreed you'd teach me, and part of that teaching must involve understanding why I'm doing the jobs you ask me to.'

Edwin threw back his head and laughed so loudly it attracted the glances of passers-by. 'God's teeth, Meg, you are fearless. I promise I will keep no more secrets if you indulge me in this one for now.'

It seemed to me that I had little alternative but to go along with Edwin's wishes. I could have refused until he explained, but then he might have decided I wasn't worth the effort. He could have found any ten-a-penny street urchin to take watch and report back to him. I liked to think he'd asked me because he trusted me, and that was an important first step to my new future. He turned to walk away, the darkness across his face again.

I called to him. 'Before you go, Edwin.'

He looked back. 'What?'

'I've found out a couple of things since we last met. You might find them interesting.'

'Tell me.'

'I saw our footman, Joseph Crowe, meet a man and almost fight with him.'

'And how is this important?'

'I challenged him later and found he'd been paying the man to return some items belonging to my mistress. The man refused and demanded more money. Joseph knew him as someone he used to drink with but claimed he hadn't seen him for an age.'

'Did you get a name?'

'Sorry, we were disturbed before I could ask

Joseph.'

'When they met, did you follow him to see where he lived?'

I looked at my feet. They shuffled as if out of my control. 'No. I was hiding from Joseph at the time, trying not to be seen. After they argued, the man ran between two cottages opposite The Antelope, but I don't know where he went.'

'No matter, Meg, we will find him. You have done well. I think you said you had found more than one thing of interest.'

I explained I'd also followed my master, and that he'd met with a woman who seemed very far beneath him.

Edwin smiled. 'This is indeed useful, though perhaps not so surprising. Men of Aubrey Beaumont's station often feel it is their right to keep a wife at home and to dally with other women whenever they feel the inclination. Taking a doxy for the night means he is satisfied and avoids the complication of maintaining a mistress of higher standing.'

I felt my cheeks begin to flush.

'Do not look so embarrassed, Meg. This is just the way of the world. Your information may come in useful, and shows you are learning this craft well. Now, you had best go back to your work and I will see you this evening.'

This time I let him leave. I had no desire to carry on this talk of my master's infidelity. Not with a man, at any rate.

I hadn't been able to concentrate on my work after Edwin asked me to meet him. I'd tried to occupy my time tidying the stables and the yard, but every minute seemed to drag by. Finally, I was able to sneak out and make my way through the town to the church where Edwin had asked me to wait. I'd been so impatient that I arrived early, meaning I had to wander round to the ruined castle to keep out of sight. Once there, I leant against its wall, warming my face in the early evening sun. Even then I couldn't settle, so I went back to the church and busied myself pulling weeds from around the gravestones. From there I could keep an eye on the two lanes and the door.

Saint Mary Magdalene's appeared a much older building than the one by Cliffe House, Saint Leonard's, and in a much poorer state of repair. My dad told of how both had been used as gunpowder stores during the war between supporters of the king and of Parliament, and both had been damaged in the fighting. The congregation of Saint Leonard's clearly cared more for the house of their Maker than worshippers at this one.

I knew none of the pious folk wandering in to vespers, though one kind gentleman stopped, thanked me for the work I was doing to keep the church tidy, and slipped me a couple of coppers. At least it seemed my play-acting was convincing.

A moment or two afterwards, Edwin appeared and peeled away from the steady stream of churchgoers to stand by the gate, glancing in every direction as he did so. One thing I soon realised was that if I put my back into working, then I couldn't keep an eye on Edwin. But if I sat gawping at him, then I'd fool no-one.

By trying to keep my head down, I missed the appearance of the man I was watching for. One minute Edwin was alone, the next, he wasn't. I'd turned my attention to a particularly stubborn dandelion root and when I looked up the man was there. Smaller than Edwin, thinner and roughly dressed, he'd his back to me so I couldn't see his face. Scooping up the weeds I'd pulled, I crept across the graveyard to seek a better view. Even from a different position, it didn't help because his face was covered.

Edwin had considered standing back in the shadows to watch for the man he was to meet, but the faithful heading to evening service would have made it difficult to pick him out. Edwin had nothing to recognise the man by. All of the churchgoers, rich and poor, looked respectable, though the time Edwin had spent in his trade had taught him not to judge by appearances. He believed there to be as many rogues in fine clothes and wigs as without, and that many with a saintly exterior hid a wicked heart beneath. The man had clearly chosen this spot well, probably knowing he would not easily stand out from the crowd. Edwin would not have discounted any of the pious making their way to church from being the person who sent the note.

He fell in place, hands folded in front, and head bowed, as if preparing to speak to his maker, and wished he could do the same so openly in his own faith. When he reached the church gate, Edwin stopped, and waited until the last worshippers made their way inside. Only one remained on the lane.

A man, thin, small in stature and poorly dressed, came from the direction of the castle ruin. His tattered scarf and down-turned hat brim hid a face in which only dark eyes were visible. He stopped a yard from Edwin and looked all around. 'You came, Mr Hare. I thought you would.'

'I had little choice, did I. What do you want?'

'Only a chat.' He made a sound halfway between a grunt and a laugh, 'for now. You could start by being nice to me.'

'Nice? Why would I be nice? I do not know you, and you send me a note with a threat. At least have the decency to tell me your name.'

'My name is not important, I have yours and that is all that matters. You may not know me, but I know much about you. I am told you killed a man. In Carlisle.'

Edwin took a step back. 'It was in battle.'

'Ay, but the one who knows told me the battle was over. And whose side were you on? I doubt you would prosper long in this town if it was known you are a Papist and supported the Young Pretender against our good King George.'

The reply did not come easily to Edwin's lips. 'So ... so what do you wish me to do about this?'

'I will give you a choice. Not an easy one, but a choice nonetheless. The man you killed was my brother. It would offer some kind of justice if you were to give yourself up to the magistrate, I believe you know him well. Explain to him what you did, and throw yourself on his mercy, though I suspect he would have none. On the other hand,' the half grunt, half laugh came again, 'my brother and I were not close, so you could pay me a quarter of your income for a year, and I will keep my mouth shut.'

Edwin leapt forward and laid a hand on the dagger at his belt. He shouted, inches away from the man's face. 'Or I could kill you.' Looking around him, he lowered his voice again. 'Not here, not now, but soon. No-one would know it was me, and I'm certain no-one would mourn your passing.'

The man backed away and raised an arm across his face, as if he still expected Edwin to attack him. 'Stay away from me, Hare, or you will regret it. Do not think I am so foolish to speak to you without considering my safety. I have a little protection hidden. Enough to keep it from prying eyes, but where it will be found easily if something happens to me. Now, you have a week to give yourself up, or to start paying me my due. Which is it to be?'

'I need time to think. If I am to confess to the magistrate, there are matters I need to deal with and to put my house in order, as I doubt I will be a free man afterwards. Believe me when I say I have known this day has been coming for a long time, when my past would return to my doorstep. Also believe me that I would much rather go to the gallows than pay the likes of you a penny piece. Meet me here again in three days and I will give you my final decision.'

The man nodded and turned to walk away towards the centre of town. He paused when Edwin touched him on the shoulder and spoke. 'In the meantime, lock your doors, stay awake, and keep a pistol cocked. I cannot be the only one who wishes you harm.'

From the graveyard I couldn't hear what was said between Edwin and the ragged man, other than when Edwin raised his voice and the words "I could kill you" couldn't be mistaken. At that point, the man stepped back and threw an arm above his face, growling something in return, then the storm passed as quickly as it came. They continued talking for a few more minutes before the man walked away, leaving Edwin standing alone, head down and shoulders slumped.

I left my hiding place and went over to him. 'What is it, Edwin? Can I help?'

He lifted his head and didn't speak immediately, peering as if trying to recognise me. 'Meg? Go, get after that devil. Find where he lives and come tell me. Go.'

I didn't need to be asked again.

The man who'd caused Edwin grief was nowhere to be seen but he'd headed off in the direction of the town. For a moment I wondered if he could have gone into one of the houses along the street, then remembered the way he'd been dressed. Hardly in keeping with the fine buildings in front of me. Beyond the church there lay nothing other than the ruined castle and the steep slopes dropping to Low Town, so he wouldn't have doubled back. I ran full tilt the way he must have gone, though kept a keen eye ahead. I did not wish to run headlong into him, nor attract his attention in some other way.

It took only a minute to spy him a hundred paces ahead, though I'd to flatten myself against a wall when he turned to look behind. I'd to repeat this again twice more before he stopped on the corner at the top of Cartway, where he looked in all directions, then removed the scarf covering his features. I cursed because he faced in the opposite direction, and I still couldn't see what he looked like.

Fortunately, there were more people on the lane downhill, and I could close the gap between us without risking being seen. Something in his build, and the way he shambled along, formed an idea that I might know who this man was after all. It was only when he approached The Antelope, and glanced back up the hill, that I could be sure. He pushed open the door of a cottage, with an alleyway between it and the next one, and my last doubt disappeared.

This man was Joseph's drinking companion from before he came to Bridgnorth. The one I'd seen him meet when he came to retrieve my mistress's goods. So why was he now meeting with Edwin?

I made sure he was inside, then knocked at his neighbour's door. A woman as old as my grandmother came out and peered down her nose at me. 'Yes?'

'Pardon me, Mistress, do you know the name of the man who lives next door?'

'Why?'

'I saw him earlier from a distance and thought he looked like my dad's friend, though wasn't certain. I've tried knocking at his door but he's not answering.'

The woman looked me up and down, as if deciding whether she should believe me or not. 'It's Steps. Ben Steps.'

Without another word she turned away and closed the door on me.

Five minutes later I tapped at Edwin's window, and he came outside. I'd never seen him looking so miserable. Though he greeted me, he didn't chat after I'd passed on the thief's name and where he lived. Instead, he, like Steps' neighbour, closed his door without a backward glance, leaving me outside, wondering what I might do next.

Eleven

The news Meg had brought the previous evening had not been good. Edwin did not know the name she'd given him, Ben Steps. This might suggest he had been told of Edwin's past by someone else.

This other person may have been more scrupulous than Steps and not prepared to use the information for gain, but Edwin would prefer it if no-one knew his secrets. He had thought when he moved here, he had left all of them behind. His allegiance to the Stuarts had faded after Culloden, and Prince Charles' flight to France. Edwin struggled to reconcile this flight with the threat posed to many good men who had fought the Prince's cause but could not flee the country to avoid retribution. Since coming south, Edwin had a new life, one in which he still practised his religion when he could, albeit clandestinely, and where he had put soldiering behind him.

His instinct was to go to find Steps, shake him a little and perhaps scare him into withdrawing his threats. Whilst this might be satisfying, he doubted it would be productive. The man had warned Edwin against violence, saying he had hidden evidence, and it would be discovered quite easily if he came to any harm. This may have been a bluff, but Edwin thought it better not to take the chance.

He tried to put away thoughts of the extortionist's demands by concentrating on Sarah Beaumont, something he had spent more and more time on in recent days. Though he was attracted to her, what did he actually know of the woman? It seemed she had arrived in Bridgnorth about the same time he had, the new wife of the magistrate. She had told him of growing up in Ludlow, of her liaison with a young man, his subsequent death, and the birth of a daughter. This was hardly enough to sustain a liaison. Before Sarah had approached him about the burglary, he had met her only a few times, and then just in passing, where she would nod, linked to her husband's elbow. They had never been properly introduced. The recent meetings where they had spoken on the street were the first time they had been together alone.

Whilst they moved in quite different social circles, the people who came to Edwin for help were often well-heeled, with valuables attractive to petty thieves, and with the money to pay for them to be recovered if stolen. One such customer, Gabriella Luca, bored and exceedingly beautiful, had pursued Edwin for a time after he had placed her swindling land agent before Aubrey Beaumont. Rumour had it that she had carried on a romantic tryst with the magistrate before he married Sarah. Some said this even continued afterwards. At the very least, the two had remained friends and, by association, Gabriella knew Sarah quite well. Edwin decided that if he wanted to know more of Sarah, Gabriella would be a good starting point.

The Luca's house was grand, though not quite so much as Aubrey Beaumont's, because it was not their main residence. This status lay with the mansion in Derbyshire, or possibly the villa outside Rome, an estate Gabriella inherited from her mother. This continued a two-hundred-year tradition of passing the property through the female line, a practice almost unthinkable in England, where a woman's wealth was forfeited as soon as she married. To Gabriella, Bridgnorth had simply been a base for her husband's business interests. She professed to like the town, though Edwin suspected she liked more the diversions provided by its male population.

Edwin had sent a calling card ahead, so the maid took him directly through to the drawing room when he arrived. Gabriella was seated facing the fire and patted the seat beside her. She raised an eyebrow when Edwin took an armchair. 'Not being a prude are we, Edwin. After all, it's not as if we are not ... friends, is it.'

'I would hope we are indeed friends, Gabriella, but with your servants in and out all the time it is better to try to be a little discrete.'

Gabriella pouted. 'Well have it your own way, my dear. To what, then, do I owe the honour of a visit? It has been a while.'

'May I count on your discretion?'

'Oh, always. This sounds fun.'

Edwin explained he had been engaged to recover some stolen goods. 'It involves an acquaintance of yours.'

Gabriella's eyebrow arched again. 'This is even better than I thought. Do tell me who.'

'Gabriella, you have to keep this to yourself. Promise?'

'I've said I will discrete have I not? You can trust me with your secrets, Edwin.'

'I need you to tell me all you know about Mrs Beaumont.'

Gabriella's eyes widened as she clasped a hand over her mouth for a split second before regaining her composure. 'Sarah? What on earth has she done?'

'I cannot tell you anything about her involvement, it would not be correct, but I do need to know of her background.'

'Well, as you are doubtless aware, I would know much more about her husband, though I will help if I can. Sarah was brought up in Ludlow, her father some kind of tradesman.'

'A cobbler, I believe.'

She waved the clarification away. 'Possibly, no matter. Not a man of Aubrey's station in any case. Aubrey could have had any woman he wanted as his wife.' Gabriella shook her head. 'Any. And yet he chose Sarah. I can only imagine he found her youth and innocence attractive.'

'Do you know how they met?'

'It is a story Aubrey likes to tell all the time. Apparently, her father had business with him, a loan of some kind. She would have been very young, and Aubrey took a fancy to her, but the father put his foot down. Even though he was heavily in Aubrey's debt, he said they could not marry until she reached her eighteenth birthday. As soon as she did, he wed her, and I expect she amused him for a while.

'It did not last though. Soon Aubrey was back to his old ways. I am sure he only keeps her for the sake of the child. That, and for the veneer of respectability she brings, of course. He may need this in the near future.'

'In what way?'

'You must know our magistrate is a man of mystery. He appeared in the town around fifteen years ago, no-one knows from where. A young man then, but seemingly a fairly rich one. Those who have known him since then say he has become less coarse than he was, though they may say this out of jealousy. Many do not like men who have made their fortune through trade. He quickly established himself with a range of businesses associated with the river. Transport, boatyards, that kind of thing, as well as the goods in demand at any one time. But the river is changing, the levels are much more variable in recent years. It is widely thought that the town's future is limited as a trading centre. I daresay Aubrey will survive, though he will need to be nimble and have strong friends around him. I shudder to think what will happen to Sarah if he loses his fortune. He would dispose of her like a shot I imagine, if he needed a rich woman to support him.'

'Did you ever hear of any affairs?'

'Aubrey? All the time.'

'Not him, his wife.'

Gabriella's laugh bordered on the cruel. 'That little mouse? Never. I do not believe she has it in her.' She paused, a thought realising itself in her eyes. 'Wait. Have you heard something? Is that what this is all about? Who on earth could she have bedded?'

Edwin held up a palm. 'Stop. You are a terrible woman, Gabriella. One moment you are saying your friend is all innocence, the next you have her an adulteress.'

'Friend? Did I say Sarah is a friend? I think not. Aubrey and I are, as I have said, ... acquainted, so she and I mix in the same circles. I have spoken to her on occasions, and one hears all kinds of tittle-tattle, but we are not close.'

'Well, as far as I am aware, Mrs Beaumont has not betrayed her husband. I merely asked if you had heard anything.'

'How sad. What a juicy morsel of gossip that would have been. I have certainly heard nothing to impugn that lady's reputation, more is the pity. I can tell you little else about her. She smiles sweetly, is pretty in an English way, and seems to manage her home well. She dotes on that daughter of hers.'

'Any close friends?'

'None I know of. As I have said, we meet some of the same people but there is not much of an overlap. Neither of us is from Bridgnorth, so not surprising I expect.

Gabriella stood, walked behind Edwin, and trailed

a finger through his hair before placing herself by the window. He wondered if she had practised taking that position to catch the light falling on her best profile.

'Now, Edwin, enough of poor Sarah. I really would like you to pay a little more attention to me.'

Two hours after Edwin had arrived at Gabriella's door, he was in a different part of the town altogether. Separated by a ten-minute walk, and a chasm of wealth and privilege, the cottages flanking Ben Steps' were not even to the standard to be found in those occupied by the servants of the Beaumonts or the Lucas. Edwin watched Steps' door for several minutes before deciding he may not be home. This and his time spent with Gabriella, turned his mind temporarily away from wishing to throttle Steps, and shifted him to considering how to recover Sarah's stolen letters without violence. The problem remained, however, of how he would silence Steps in the matter of his own past.

From higher up the lane, a bald man puffed down the hill holding the reins of a hungry-looking donkey. This beast was the deepest black, with a golden snout. Its most outstanding feature was the red fur lining its pricked-up ears. The beast appeared to be nudging its handler all the way down the road, before they came to rest two doors away from Steps' home, when the man deftly threw the reins over a hook fixed in the cottage wall.

The donkey's owner approached his door and was

set to go inside until Edwin called to him. 'Excuse me, sir, could you help?'

The man stopped and placed his hands on his hips. 'I'll do my best, as long as it don't require me to spend any money, nor keep away from my dinner for long.'

'I think I can fulfil both of those requirements Mister ...'

'Roe, Marcus Roe, at your service.'

'Well Mr Roe, I am looking for a man, name of Ben Steps, I've been told he lives down here.'

Roe spat on the ground. 'He does. More's the pity.' He pointed to Steps' cottage. 'That one there.'

'You are not a friend then?'

'With him? I'd hope not. You can see that none who live here are wealthy, quite the opposite, but we are honest in the main. Not that man. He would steal the coat from your back and then try to sell it back to you. A bad lot, a real bad lot. I beg your pardon, sir, if you're acquainted or related, but I have to speak my mind.'

'Put any concerns on that score to rest, Mr Roe. Steps is no friend of mine. Would you know where he is at present?'

'At this time of day, he will as likely as not be found in the Black Boy tavern, down below. If he's not there cooking up a scheme, then he will be engaged on one and I can't guess where that might be.'

'What kind of scheme does he take on then?'

'Anywhere money might be made. Thieving. Burglary. Even extorting money some would say.'

'Extortion?'

'Indeed. Steps'll find some secret or other and

torture a poor soul until they pay for him to keep it to himself. I'd think the man has many enemies.'

'So, he is wealthy?'

'Not at all, at least not as far as I can tell. He spends every penny drinking and playing dice in the tavern.' Roe stopped in his tracks. 'But I've already said more than enough and my stomach's crying for want of food. I must bid you good day.'

Roe did not wait for a reply and went inside without another word, leaving Edwin in the lane trying to decide if he should try another neighbour or wait until another day. From the corner of his eye, he sensed movement at a window on the opposite side so walked over knocked gently at the door. He received no reply, so tapped harder, with the same result.

Edwin had called on my master again in the early afternoon. I don't know if he had business with the magistrate, or if he wanted his visit to disguise speaking to me. In the light of what I'd seen over recent days, he may have just wanted to catch a glimpse of Mrs Beaumont again. Whatever the real reason, he'd beckoned me over when he saw me in the garden.

'Meg. I am busy for the rest of the day and need you to speak to some men for me. They are fences. You know what that is?'

I snorted. 'Of course. It's a man who buys and sells stolen goods.'

'Excellent.' He handed me a small sheet of paper.

'Then I want you to take this message to each of them and enquire about a locket and a cloak fastening.'

'Why would they tell me?'

'Because it's not you asking, it's me. And if they are wise, they won't cross me. These men tend not to be too brave. They are businessmen at heart, without the stomach for outright thievery, or for time spent in gaol. They all know I could get them hanged for their crimes with little effort.'

Edwin told me the names of the men I was to talk to, and where I would find them. He also gave me descriptions of the items I was to look for, and repeated them three times, just to make sure I'd remember.

I said I wouldn't be able to get away until early evening when my work was done, but he answered this would be fine, and I should report back to him when I could.

Later, after I'd wolfed down my broth, bread, and cheese, I slipped out of the stables and made my way to the first on his list, Jeremiah Bell. I showed him the note Edwin had written, simple enough for any man to understand. *This girl is working for me. Tell her anything she asks.*

Bell squinted and ran a bony finger across the words twice, his lips forming the words. He clicked his tongue and handed it back.

I'd never been in such a room as his. Other than one chair, a rough table and the hearth, there were no furnishings. Against each wall were stacked every manner of items. Boxes, large and small, bags, muskets, tools, paintings, fine clothing, footwear, and periwigs.

The fence looked me up and down. 'I suppose I must trust you have not forged this?'

'Don't judge everyone by your own standards, Mr Bell, I'd have no use for any information you can offer. I'm just a humble gardener sent on an errand by the thief-taker. So will you answer his questions or not?'

'Ask away, lady. I owe Edwin Hare too many favours to refuse him this one.'

'He wants to know if you've been offered a locket. Gold, on a chain, possibly with a few strands of blond hair inside. Not precious, except to the one who's lost it. Also, a fine clasp for a cloak.'

'When would this be?'

'Didn't say, though I think it'd be in the last thirty days.'

'Then I must disappoint you, and Hare.' Bell turned and scrabbled away in a corner, pulling a box from a pile. He flipped it open to reveal a hoard of small items of jewellery. 'Here is what I have, there are no clasps. I have lockets but none came so recently into my possession. And I have not disposed of anything such as you describe. Not in many a month.'

'You're sure?'

'Why would I lie? Hare knows my trade and that it would be too dangerous for me to withhold the truth from him. He could have me before the magistrate in the blink of an eye. Instead, he allows me to continue to earn a crust in my simple way, in exchange for snippets of information when he needs them.'

I thanked Bell for his time and made my way to the next name on my list, the second of three.

So it was with him too, a similar box of trinkets but not the ones we sought. The third man, Caleb Capstick, was no more forthcoming, though I'd have trusted him the least. Even so, he professed to be hiding nothing, and that it wouldn't be worth his while to lie to Edwin.

I marvelled at the openness and dishonesty of these men, part of a system of thieves and robbers, none of whom could trust the others. Even the rogue who they sold their cargo to, at a quarter of its real value, would expose them to the law if it suited his ends.

Disappointed I'd not been able to find anything to help in Edwin's search, and because I didn't believe the man, I tried another direction with Capstick. I made as if my business for Edwin had finished and looked around me before lowering my voice to a whisper. 'I must tell you, sir, I want some jewellery myself, if you've anything a poor woman as me could afford. A simple necklace perhaps?'

Capstick rubbed his hands and chuckled.

'I am sure we can find you something.'

He searched for a moment before grabbing a small sack and emptying the tangled contents on the table, a bird's nest of gold and silver. I felt my eyes widen. 'Would any of these suit you, madam?'

As he spoke, a look of panic appeared and, when I looked from his face back at the jewels before us, I immediately saw the cause. Shining out from the middle of the pile lay a locket just like the one I'd described. The fool had clearly forgotten which hiding place he'd stored it in. I lifted it out and dangled its chain from one finger. 'So, what do we have here, Mr Capstick? Isn't this the trinket I asked about?'

The man made to run, then whether realising he was in his own house, or knowing Edwin would easily find him, he stopped and scowled. 'Ah, so it is. I had quite forgotten, though I am quite certain I have seen no clasp.'

He must have known this pretence wouldn't work but I had to allow him to save face if I was to learn anything further. 'Quite easily done, Mr Capstick, it must be so difficult to remember everything in your possession, especially as none of it actually belongs to you. Now you've seen it, can you remember who sold you the locket?'

The name he gave wasn't unexpected. Ben Steps. But I couldn't think why my mistress would be so upset at the loss of such a trinket, nor why she'd ask Joseph to pay a decent sum of money to get it back. Perhaps it wasn't the item she wanted most.

Twelve

Edwin ambled down St Mary's Street, away from his cottage. Above him, in the town, the bells of St Leonard's were calling its congregation to the Sunday morning service, by far the best attended of the week. The couples he met on the street all walked in that direction. Several nodded or offered a word of greeting. One or two eyed him as if to ask why he too was not going to speak with his Lord. Edwin smiled at the thought and wondered what their reaction would be if they knew that he was, their God and his God were only two faces of the same one, split by King Henry VIII, two hundred years earlier.

At the bottom of the slope, Edwin passed through the ruined Hungary Gate in what was left of the town walls, then turned to climb the hill. The path levelled at the top, where it meandered through a birch coppice, the boundary of a farm owned by Gabriella Luca's husband, before opening to a yard with a brick and timber barn at the far end. The Lucas being great benefactors of the Catholic church, their land and properties throughout the region provided many secret meeting places for followers of their faith, this barn being one.

Five men and three women stood outside. Edwin recognised them all from previous occasions. One, in a black robe and white collar, broke away from the group and greeted him warmly. 'Edwin, I am pleased you have been able to join us.'

'Good morning, Father, and I am pleased to be here. You had a good journey?'

The priest smiled. 'Good is perhaps taking it a little too far. Taxing but fulfilling might be more apt. Meeting the faithful in towns and villages between Derby and here was deeply satisfying. The secrecy and fear of discovery, less so.

'On the good side, in Stafford I met a priest recently returned from Rome. He carried news that Prince Charles may be assembling a force in France for another invasion.'

Edwin grimaced. 'Father, it's barely three years since the rout at Culloden and he fled for the Continent. I cannot believe his followers have the stomach for another fight.'

'They ... you ... have to, Edwin. It is only through a Stuart restoration that the Catholic faith has any chance left on these islands.' The priest pointed a thumb at the barn behind him. 'How long can we continue to worship like this? How long can we face meeting with no more than five allowed to share our prayers? No matter our station in life, wealthy or poor, we are excluded from all positions of authority. A man such as you could be anything you want, but you're forbidden by virtue of faith.'

'That would be the case, Father, if my faith were known. It is not, and I hope to keep it so. The good Lord knows I am of the true faith; I do not need my neighbours to know. Now, let us go inside to reduce the chances of them finding out.'

Edwin bowed his head to the priest and made his way to join the others. Whilst he had been talking, the group had been joined by Gabriella and her husband, who nodded and accompanied him into the barn. She, as always, dressed like a queen, and he, Vincente, whilst less flamboyant, still wore a fashion more reminiscent of the Italian Court than a lowly town in Shropshire.

The overwhelming smell of hay and horses caused Edwin and his companions to catch their breath, and Gabriella to lift the pouncet box hanging on its gold chain from her waist. She wafted it beneath her nose then released her husband's arm when the fresh orange peel took effect.

Vincente Luca spoke to Edwin for the first time. 'Why we continue to meet in these places, Mr Hare, I do not understand. In my country we have the most beautiful churches in the world, dripping with gold and fabulous artworks, every one built to the glory of God. A God we are free to worship whenever and wherever we please.'

'For this I envy you, sir, but some would say the good Lord was born in a stable such as this, so we should be grateful to see the world as He first saw it.'

'You do not believe this, Mr Hare, surely? It sounds

like the ravings of your Protestant countrymen.'

Edwin laughed. 'No, I do not, it is but an argument to get me through the morning and to tolerate the stench of this place. I would much rather we were in one of your fine buildings, where the smells are sweet, and the horses are where they would be better suited - tied up outside.' He swung a hand towards the bales of straw facing the portable altar brought by their priest. 'Shall we take our seats?'

Thirteen

With Hannah finally asleep in her cot, Sarah looked up from the note on her bedroom windowsill and surveyed the garden. In summer, when trees were in full growth, she would see little from this position, but now, with most of the leaves gone, it was laid out in full view. Bordering the terrace, the roses still provided a little colour, lifting them from the evergreen hedges of the parterre. In a section beyond the kitchen garden wall, only visible from her room, the rows of vegetables and fruit promised a good winter store. Beyond this, the land fell away, quarter of a mile to the river out of sight below, rising again to the wooded hills beyond the valley. The low, late afternoon sun edged all the features of the garden in gold, bringing a sense of magic.

Her eyes caught the methodical movement of Meg Valentine, the girl digging and turning the soil, bending occasionally to lift an errant weed and toss it into her barrow. A kind of physical poetry, each movement just sufficient and no more. Sarah's mind lingered on this scene, finding a calm she hadn't felt for days.

If only the problems in her own life could be disposed of so easily. She'd hoped to achieve this by sending Joseph to her torturer, but the footman had paid over her last remaining funds and only returned with a demand for more. The young man had seemed so upset she could only feel sorry for him, though it did not help her cause.

Edwin Hare had sent the name of the thief the previous afternoon, having asked Joseph to deliver it into her hand. Seeing the footman appearing much calmer, she had taken the opportunity to press him about the man she had sent him to bargain with. He confirmed the name and told her where he lived. Despite her doubts about Joseph's possible involvement in the theft, his contriteness pushed her to give him some leniency. Not that she had much choice, she could hardly go to Aubrey and demand his footman's dismissal.

She remained watching the gardener until her anxiety bubbled up again. Sarah paced the room for a minute or two then lay on her bed, staring at the ceiling. Her brain told her to simply let Edwin Hare deal with Steps, but her anger prodded her to approach the extortionist herself and try to reason with him. She had no more money to give, not even enough to pay the thief-taker for his services so far. Begging Steps for mercy may be her only reasonable option. Were there other, unreasonable, ones?

It took a full half hour for Sarah to arrive at her decision before she rose, changed her clothes for the task in hand, and went downstairs to speak to her maid. 'I need to go out for a short while, Polly, please listen for Hannah to wake, then feed her and sit with her until I return.'

The girl nodded without comment and went back to her duties, leaving Sarah with one more item to collect before leaving the house.

The boots proved an apt choice as Sarah picked her way through the mud and muck of Cartway. Despite slipping and sliding, she kept her hand on the dagger inside her cloak and held her head down, even though shadows had already spread across the narrow lane. Sarah kept to the opposite side when she approached the Antelope tavern, where drunken singing spilled out through the half-door. As she passed, the singing stopped, and angry shouting erupted. She quickened her step at the sound of a crash from inside.

At Ben Steps' cottage, Sarah glanced in both directions and around the windows of surrounding buildings. Satisfied she was not being observed, she knocked.

A bolt was pulled back, the door opened, and Steps peered out, screwing up his eyes even further to take in the face beneath the hood. 'Oh, it's you, madam. Come in. I've been expecting you.'

As Sarah did so, gripping the handle of her weapon even tighter, she spied a woman's pale face peeking from a door across the street and, from the shadows on the corner, a thin man quietly watching silently

Inside, Steps swiped the dust from a chair with a rough cloth and with an exaggerated wave of his hand offered a seat to his visitor.

She shook her head. 'No thank you, I shall not be staying long. Our business will be concluded quickly.'

'Please yourself, Mrs Beaumont. I take it you've brought more money.'

The use of her name unnerved Sarah for a second, though she replied strongly.

'Indeed, I have not. What I sent earlier was our bargain. You should have returned my papers with my footman.'

Steps laughed. A cruel sound, with no mirth. 'It's clear you don't grasp the situation, Mrs Beaumont. The price I asked was just to see if you'd pay anything, and you quickly took the bait. If you'd waited longer, or offered less, I'd have had doubts about the value of your goods. Now I know your items are worth much more to you than I could have hoped. The price of the goods has gone up. At least twice as much. What do you think?'

Whilst he had been speaking, Sarah had looked Steps up and down. She was not tall, nor particularly strong, but neither was the man before her. If she moved quickly, she might have the better of him.

Sarah leapt forward and pushed him against the wall. She pulled the dagger from beneath her cloak and pressed its tip under Steps' chin. 'I am afraid it is you who do not understand, Mr Steps. The letters you stole *are*, as you say, important. Important enough for me to go to any lengths to get them back,' she forced the point harder, causing a rivulet of blood to trickle towards her clenched fingers, 'any lengths at all.'

Edwin walked casually, like a man at ease with the world, a man with no intent other than to take the evening air. If this had been true, of course, he would have chosen a route with less stench than this. Sadly, that would not have taken him where he wanted to go. Cartway was quiet, which suited him, and the evening shadows had lengthened, providing him with cover on the narrow lane. Edwin was aware they would also hide anyone who might be watching.

If there had been any lingering doubt about Matthew Kemp having been involved in the theft from Cliffe House, it had disappeared earlier in the day when a pedlar fresh from Ludlow brought Edwin a message from the man's employer, Barnabus Child. The reply was courteous and not only confirmed that Kemp had been sent to Leominster as he had said, but reported that he was the most honest of men. Mr Child took great pains to explain his employee had been in a position of considerable trust for some time and had always shown correctness and integrity in their dealings. Edwin had thought it unlikely Kemp could be involved, but was pleased the matter had been settled, and his instinct had proved correct.

On arriving at Steps' door, he found it slightly ajar. He resisted the temptation to push his way inside unannounced. Instead, he knocked and waited. When no answer came, he knocked again, then pushed the door open enough to be heard. 'Mr Steps?'

Edwin thought his voice was clear, but no-one answered. He stepped into a room even sparser than his own. A table, a chair, a cupboard, and a fire dying in the grate. In the darkness of the corner, Ben Steps lay on his bed.

Minutes later, Edwin slipped out again, pulled the door to the position he had found it when he arrived, and pressed his back against the cottage wall so he would not be seen. He pulled his hat brim down and his coat collar up.

When his breathing slowed, he strode back up the hill, keeping to the shadows until he turned the corner at the top. Only then he pressed a hand to his chest, making sure the letters were still in his inside pocket.

John Latewood strained to hold back his load on the steep Cartway as he trudged up from the riverside, for the tenth time since morning. He winced as his knee clicked. An oath escaped his lips, part with the pain and part at needing to call on Ben Steps to pay his weekly due. In past times he'd have left his cart at the bottom of the hill, ready for his climb home, but the rumours he'd heard that day convinced him it would be stolen before he returned. Tales were all around the riverbank of thefts from the wharfs and the boats, not to mention word of a highwayman holding up travellers on the roads outside the town. John had looked for a friendly face, someone he could trust to look after his cart, with no luck. All the river traders had long gone, tied up and most enjoying Michaelmas in the gin house. He spoke to some friends standing outside The Black Boy, but they were away home for their supper and unwilling to look after his cart until the morning. This part of Bridgnorth would only attract lowlife to its lanes and paths for the next few hours.

Mindful of this, Latewood paused in the deeper shadow when he turned a bend and saw a figure push open Steps' door and go inside. He watched a while until the person emerged again. In the darkness all he caught was a flash of skin beneath a hood, not enough to recognise, even though the face looked briefly in his direction. The carter quickly leaned into the shadows, pretending to pee. He did not want to meet anyone on this errand, it was bad enough that Steps knew his secret, without people wondering why he might be calling on a known rogue.

In the great scheme of things, he considered his wrongdoing had been a minor one, even if condemned by the church and the law. He believed it would be pardoned by anyone he might call a friend. Latewood's wife had been a shrew, always berating him, and occasionally beating him. So, he had left her far behind upriver and taken another. He felt he had done nothing wrong, but still knew he would need to pay Steps when he came calling last spring.

Whilst the bigamist carter thought of these things, the person turned and slunk away up the hill. Latewood stepped out and looked after them. Man? Woman? He could not be sure. The clothing favoured a man, but the hood and cloak hiding the person's features made it easy for disguise. The dark clothing merging into the dusk also made it difficult to gauge the height and physique of the rapidly disappearing figure. Rumour had it Steps had a number of poor souls under his control, men and women alike, so his visitor could have been any one of them.

Waiting until he was sure the person was not returning, Latewood checked the lane for anyone else, then left his cart and made his way over to Steps' cottage. He glanced once more up and down Cartway and ducked inside.

The room was dark, other than the dimmest glimmer from the hearth. 'Master Steps? You here?'

No answer returned.

His fifty years told Latewood he should leave and return in daylight, but his curiosity got the better of him, alongside a vague thought that if Steps was out, it might be possible to find and retrieve the evidence which Steps held against him. He waited for a minute until his eyes grew accustomed to the gloom, then saw two things. Firstly, he spotted a cupboard in a corner with three drawers above, all of them pulled out. The second was a foot, poking from beneath a blanket, not naked as might be expected, but still booted.

Latewood thought again that he should go, and again he denied his own better sense and took two steps forward.

His tormentor lay glassy eyed on the bed, looking for all the world like he was simply taking a nap, apart from the dark halo of blood around his head. It had seeped from the gaping slash to his throat.

This time Latewood listened to what his brain was telling him and ran headlong into the street, bawling for help. For Ben Steps, though, there was no help to be had.

A child ran up the coroner's path and hammered on his door. Though I couldn't hear what was said, there was no mistaking the look of concern on the face of the footman, nor the urgency with which the servant returned inside.

After work, Dad had sent me to drop off some spare vegetables to an old woman he knew to be recently widowed and fallen on hard times. Going home, I was passing Doctor Lewis Perry's house. I'd been in no hurry, so hung around and only had to wait two or three minutes to see the coroner leave. He walked as fast as his considerable stomach and short legs would allow him, in the direction of the market place. Dr Perry's servant followed hard at his heels, carrying a large leather bag in one hand and a ledger under his arm. I'd no need to hide my pursuit of them, for I wasn't the only one who noticed their passing and thought there must be something interesting going on. Soon I was in the middle of a stream of men and women with nothing better to do, and with a want for entertainment.

The evening had turned chill after dark, and the sound of the crowd, murmuring and stamping feet to keep warm, told me something was amiss on Cartway, even before I turned the corner halfway down the hill.

Twenty or more people were round Ben Steps' door by the time I arrived, others joining with each passing minute from lower down. These ranks were swelled by those arriving with me. I pushed my way through the first ring for a better view, though there wasn't much more to be seen, despite the lamps some onlookers had brought with them.

All around, people were passing the news, or at least their version of it. The general story seemed to be that commotion from a man called John Latewood had raised the alarm.

I spoke to a man of about my own age beside me. 'What's happened?'

'Murder, by the sound of it.'

'Of Ben Steps?'

'You know him?'

The caution in his voice made me remember to be careful what I revealed. 'Only that he lives here. He was known to a friend, that's all. How about you?'

'He's a neighbour ... or was,' the man pointed a thumb over his shoulder, 'I live on that side with my parents. I don't think I know you, though.'

'Perhaps not. I'm Meg, I work for Mr Beaumont up by Saint Leonard's.'

'The magistrate? Pleased to meet you, Meg. I am Peter.'

The twinkle in his eye told me he wasn't simply being polite. This dark-haired, brown-eyed, Peter, was handsome, with a sturdy frame, but I'd need to enquire more about his prospects in life before returning his interest. 'So, Peter, what have you heard?'

He told me one brave person had gone inside to check what Latewood had seen, and when it was clear Steps hadn't gone to meet his Maker naturally, a child was sent to fetch the Coroner.

Peter pointed to a man in the crowd. 'My father there said the good doctor would only usually deal with bodies of people who'd died of sickness and old age, so wouldn't often need to leave his premises. It's only when there's been an accident, where someone other than the dead person's to blame, or cases like Steps', that the Coroner comes out before allowing the corpse to be removed.'

All this talk of corpses made me shiver, though I felt both a thrill and disgust at the same time. I asked him if he knew what would happen next. He shook his head. A woman beside us, who'd clearly been earwigging, cackled and said it would be a great fun for a few days. Though I thought this ghoulish, it wasn't a hundred miles away from the way I felt.

The crowd had begun to grow restless while we waited. A few left, doubtless deciding there'd be no more excitement to keep them from their homes, but mostly people muttered to one another and shuffled their feet. From the back, one man shouted there was a killer loose and the coroner should be quick about his business. Eventually the door opened again, and Doctor Perry emerged.

A cry went up and he raised his hand to quieten it. 'Good people. I have to tell you some evil has taken place here this evening.' A rumble of gasps, like distant thunder, rippled through the air. 'The man who lived in this cottage has been most foully murdered, his throat cut. It cannot have happened too many hours ago so the villain may still be nearby. Have any of you seen anything suspicious?'

Peter leant in and whispered in my ear. 'Steps himself was suspicious. Not surprising he has met a bad end if you ask me. People always coming and going, and none with a smile on their face.'

A voice just behind me cried out 'Dr Perry! You should ask John Latewood. He found the body'

The coroner spoke to his clerk, then turned back to the crowd. 'John Latewood? Are you here?'

A man, grey-faced and shaking, stepped forward. 'I'm Latewood.'

A whisper ran round before Dr Perry replied. 'Did you see anything, sir?'

'You mean other than that villain with his throat cut?' This time a gasp from the crowd.

'Yes. Did you see anyone leaving or on the street?'

'There was someone. Left the cottage just before I got there.'

'Man or woman?'

'Couldn't tell, sir. All covered up they was. Dark as well.'

'And you made no attempt to stop them?'

Latewood snorted. 'Why would I do such a thing? Was glad I didn't when I saw what they'd done to Steps. Could have stabbed me as well.'

The crowd roared with laughter until the coroner

raised his hand again.

'Then you must go to the magistrate in the morning and tell him all that you saw.' He turned back to address the assembly. 'There is nothing more to be done this night. I will convene a Coroner's Court at The Crown at the proper time and will call some of you as witnesses to determine how this poor soul met his end. Now, please go home to your beds whilst my man and I attend to Mr Steps.'

I expected there to be further uproar but there was none. The crowd turned, almost in unison, and spread in all directions, like a pile of leaves in a sudden gust of wind, leaving only Peter and I, and a bald man who moved towards a door close to Steps' own, then appeared to change his mind and approached Doctor Perry instead. I heard his words clearly.

'My name is Marcus Roe, sir.' He pointed to a door two away from Steps. 'I live there and saw no-one tonight, but two days ago a man came asking questions about Ben Steps. I don't know his name but would recognise him again. Should I tell this to the magistrate?'

The coroner nodded, affirming that he should, and the man returned to his home.

Peter turned his attention back to me. 'So, we have a mystery. As I said, any one of ten men and women would like to see the end of Steps. It'll be hard to unravel who hated him most. Enough to plunge a knife into his throat'

'Indeed it will.'

As I spoke, two thoughts sprung to my mind. One,

that the man asking questions would be Edwin, without doubt. The other thought was that I liked my new friend Peter very much.

Fourteen

Gabriella led Edwin from her drawing room through to an orangery overlooking the garden. He had never seen this strange fruit growing anywhere else and had only tasted a segment once. He lifted a ripe orange and breathed in its scent deeply. He released it, so as not to allow it to drop from the plant, and continued to hold his hand to his nose, inhaling the mystery.

Sarah had arrived before him and rose to greet him, then sat again when their host spoke directly to Edwin. 'You have but half an hour, Edwin, not a minute longer. If my husband, Vincente, returns and finds either of you here there will be questions to be answered. Questions none of us would like to address. I have sent my maid on an errand so you will remain undisturbed. And undiscovered. Also, let me make this abundantly clear. I will not extend this courtesy again. Do you understand?'

Edwin grimaced. 'I do, Gabriella, and if I could have arranged a meeting without your involvement I would have done so. You have my gratitude.'

She fluttered a hand, as if to say it was of little

consequence, then left.

Edwin took a seat by Sarah and pulled a small bundle from within his coat. 'I believe these are yours, Mrs Beaumont.'

Sarah drew a deep breath, her hand shaking as she leaned across to take it from him. She peeled back the well-worn sheet of paper enclosing her letters and leafed through them, finally lifting one to her face to take in the scent of it.

As she did so, Edwin put a hand in his pocket, bringing it out with fingers folded to his palm. He gestured for Sarah to open her hand, and he dropped a gold locket into her palm.

A tear escaped her eye. 'What? How?'

Edwin grinned. 'It was nothing. Steps sold them on, and my helper found who had bought them.'

'This is much, much, more than nothing, sir. These precious mementos mean the world, and their exposure would have ruined me. I do not know how to repay you.'

'Repayment need only be my standard fee, madam, as we agreed. In some cases, I take a percentage of the value of goods recovered. With items such as these, I would be no better than the man who stole them if I tried to profit from their recovery. I will take no more for myself than to cover the time I have spent in searching for them. There will need to be a little added to compensate the man who bought your keepsake, perhaps not in good faith but at least in the way of business. I would also not have found the culprit so quickly without his assistance. His payment will be much less than the extra I would have needed to charge for more time. Sadly, he did not have the clasp which was taken, and I have been unable to locate anyone who does.'

'That does not matter, Mr Hare. It is valuable but was only a gift from my husband and he can buy me another. The other items are worth much more to me. If you are sure that this will be sufficient then I will pay you tomorrow. Will this be acceptable?'

Edwin stiffened, 'I had hoped we could settle straight away, Mrs Beaumont, I may need to leave Bridgnorth quickly, and you have seen how difficult it is for us to meet without eyebrows being raised.'

'I am afraid I had not expected you to have dealt with the matter so soon, consequently brought no money with me when I left home today. I apologise sincerely. If we should meet tomorrow morning at ten o'clock? Perhaps by chance, as we did last time, then I am sure I will be able to give you what you ask.'

'Then this will have to do. I believe I may be passing your glove supplier at about that time.'

'Thank you for your understanding, Mr Hare.'

Sarah paused for a moment. 'I have been considering if Joseph might have been involved in some way.'

'I wouldn't be surprised. The two knew each other.'

'Joseph knew this man Steps?'

'He did, I understand they had been friends before Joseph entered your husband's employment.'

'So is this how this ... creature knew where to find my letters?'

'I do not know yet. I will ask him as soon as I am able. Perhaps we may talk about this more when we meet tomorrow.'

It didn't take long for my question about Edwin's involvement in Steps' death to be answered. He sent a message with Joseph that he needed to see me at around eleven o'clock in the market place.

Joseph had been in a tavern the previous night and was full of the news of Steps murder, though, in the telling, the story had grown from a slit throat to dismemberment. Rather than a single killer, as yet unknown, it had become a conspiracy of all those the man had wronged over the years. Joseph even had the audacity to ask me, in a whisper, if I thought our mistress might be involved.

I laughed off the accusation, though both of us knew Steps had a hold over her. My own mind was still full of Edwin's possible involvement.

At the appointed time I waited for Edwin, and he arrived not a minute late according to St Leonard's bell.

His manner was most disturbed, with his eyes watching constantly in all directions, and more than a little edginess in his voice. 'The business with your mistress is now concluded, Meg, though I cannot say more and cannot pay you at the moment. I may need to go from the town for a period, but I will send what I owe as soon as I can.'

I was about to reply that I wanted no payment,

when a cry went up from a bald man unloading a cart on to a stall. He was pointing in our direction. 'Stop! Murderer! There, that's him. The one asking about Ben Steps. Stop him.'

Edwin made to run, but the crowd was around us in a flash. He set himself for a fight then saw were too many, so he held up his hands. 'I will not resist. You may take me to the magistrate, but I did not kill anyone. Please let my friend here go on her way, she has nothing to do with this and merely stopped to speak in passing.'

I looked at him to protest but he shook his head and waved me away. 'Go, Meg, you have no further part to play in this affair. I work for Mr Beaumont often, and we will have this sorted out in no time. When we have, I will be in touch.'

The crowd parted to let me through, one rank at a time, each closing afterwards, so I had no view of Edwin after the first. There was no need for me to follow when they moved off. I knew their destination and would be there before them.

'You were seen, Hare. Asking questions about the murdered man only hours before he is found dead. Later, another witness saw someone slipping out of Steps' door. They said it could have been you.'

Aubrey Beaumont looked across his desk at Edwin, who he had told to remain standing, though the ignominy of guards had been dispensed with.

'You know none of this signifies anything, Mr

Beaumont, I ask about people every day. It is my job, and I do much of it on your behalf.'

'You do, but this was not a case I had asked you to examine though, was it?'

'No, it was not, an individual who had been wronged asked for my help and I gave it.'

'May I ask who it was?'

'I am afraid it would be imprudent to say.'

'Imprudent? You are accused of a crime here, man, a serious one, it is not the time for scruples.'

'Nonetheless, I am not prepared to say who engaged me. As for your second witness, "could have been you" is not good enough. If he or she cannot identify the person leaving, then it could have been anyone. One thing is for certain though, it was not me. What about this carrier who supposedly found the body?'

'I have spoken to ...' the magistrate consulted a note, 'this John Latewood and though he admits to making regular payments to the victim there is no way he killed the man. Ten minutes before he arrived by Steps' door, he was talking to friends lower down the hill. He was also in a serious condition of mind when I spoke to him. The man has far too nervous a disposition to put a knife in someone's throat.'

A shout came from outside and the magistrate walked over to the window.

'There is a mob by my gate, Hare, baying for your blood. Am I to give you to them? By all accounts this Steps fellow was most unsavoury, but this does not stop the townspeople wanting justice to be done. At least tell me why you were asking his neighbours about him.'

'A person of some note, who will remain anonymous, asked me to recover some items of value. My enquiries led me to Steps' door, but he was not home when I called on him. I therefore took the opportunity to find out what I could about the man. As you suggest, he was a villain and tormentor to many folk who will not be unhappy to see him gone.'

Beaumont pulled a face and rubbed his chin. 'Then what am I to do? I cannot just let you go, that rabble outside would stone my house and attack my servants.'

'Release me on condition I find Ben Steps' killer. That should satisfy them.'

'And what if you do not?'

'Give me a week and I will have the person responsible in your custody. If I fail, then you must deal with me as you see fit.'

The magistrate shook his head. 'You must think me a fool, Hare. You could travel a long time in a week, well beyond any power I may have to bring you back.'

'Then I will report to you twice every day, once in the morning and once in the afternoon. That way, if I was to run, which I will not, it would be an easy chase for the men you send after me. Could you live with this arrangement?'

Beaumont looked out of the window again before replying. 'I expect I can. It will also give an opportunity for you to let me know what progress you are making. Now, I must have words with those people and let them know my decision. If they do not like it, I will need to call out the militia to have them dispersed. Let us hope it does not come to that; I want no blood on *my* hands.'

Edwin called on Aubrey Beaumont a little after half past nine, as he had promised, explained he would begin his investigations directly, then left. He hoped to catch Sarah Beaumont on her route to their planned rendezvous. This would enable him to effect the most natural of meetings, offering to accompany her on her morning walk. He was out of luck, though she *was* waiting for him at the glove shop when he arrived. They made their greetings as before and started a casual stroll through the town.

Sarah spoke so she would not be overheard. 'I saw you at my home yesterday. Aubrey said there had been some trouble. A killing I believe?'

'Ben Steps, the man who stole your letters.'

'Oh, my goodness, Aubrey did not mention the victim's name. I am not sorry to hear it. Horrible person. Have they caught the man who did it?'

'It is not known if it was a man or a woman, there are no witnesses of note, but your husband believes it was me.'

'You? Why would you want to kill the man? Unless it was to gain favour with me?'

'Do not raise yourself so high, madam. I may welcome your attentions, but I would not kill a man to receive them.'

'So you *would* welcome them?'

Edwin coughed. 'Is there a gentleman who wouldn't? But that is of little importance, is it, you are a married woman, and we are only here to discuss payment of your bill.'

'The two are not necessarily unconnected, sir.'

'I am sorry, but I fail to understand.'

'Then if I must spell the letters out, I must. I am afraid I lied to you yesterday. In fact, the issue of your fee has vexed me since we first spoke. I have no money of my own, at least none I can spare, and I cannot ask my husband for any. At least not for this purpose. You must see this?'

Edwin nodded.

The lady paused; her eyes lowered. 'I have nothing I can offer to you except myself.'

Sarah left the statement hanging in the air, watching for Edwin's reaction. She turned away briefly and acknowledged a customer of her husband's who had greeted her. Returning to Edwin she lowered her tones again. 'Well? Would such a bargain be of any interest?'

Edwin's response was a hiss, the shout he wished to make constrained by the need to avoid drawing attention. 'Any other time, I may jump at the opportunity, madam, and I am much flattered by your suggestion, but at this juncture I need hard cash. I may need to escape Bridgnorth, possibly even Shropshire. And in any case, what you offer seems to be given away too cheaply to be of any real value.'

Sarah swung on him in a flash, her palm almost

connecting with his cheek before Edwin parried, grabbing her wrist, and pushing it down to her side. He glared for a moment before letting go and walking quickly away, cursing under his breath.

Fifteen

The household was full of the news of Edwin being taken in to the master for the killing of Ben Steps and that he had been released only on condition he catch the real murderer if it was not him. Opinion was divided as to whether it was him or not, because rumour was rife. Joseph told me he had heard in the tavern, where, of course, the truth is always told, that the thief-taker had been seen, clear as day, carrying a knife with blood dripping from its blade. Mrs Beaumont's maid, Polly, who I think is more than a little sweet on Edwin, claimed he had been witnessed leaving the residence of the Italian lady, Mrs Luca, at the same time the carter found Steps' body.

For my part, I couldn't decide. I believed Edwin could be capable of killing a man, but perhaps not in cold blood. In my heart I wished him not to be guilty because this would put paid to my plans to carve out a profitable career in his footsteps. I knew this was selfish but couldn't help it.

I missed the opportunity to speak with him on the first morning he came to see Mr Beaumont, though followed closed behind when he left. Watching from the safety of the ironmonger's yard, I was not much surprised when he met with my mistress. They seemed to be talking in a casual way until she tried to strike him and he stalked off.

He headed straight towards my hiding place, so I stepped out. 'Morning, Edwin, I didn't expect to see you in the marketplace so early.'

He scowled for a moment, then responded to my smile. 'It is not by choice, Meg, I had errands to run and, as I am sure you have heard by now, I have a murder to unravel.'

'I'd heard this, Edwin. Anything I can do?'

'Thank you, but no. Not at the minute. There is news on the other matter though. I have managed to retrieve the stolen items and returned them to their rightful owner, your mistress, so I can pay you what you are due on that account. I have not the money with me, so will meet you in half an hour at Whelan's coffee house where we can settle up. If you arrive before me, please order a drink, and tell Whelan I will be there directly.'

I protested that there was no need for payment, but Edwin insisted he always met his debts, so I agreed to see him as he asked. He went in the direction of his home, leaving me wondering what excuse I could give to my master if he discovered my absence.

The coffee house was almost empty. Edwin had told me it was where men got together to discuss the comings and goings of the town, make trades, or cultivate contacts. I assumed it must still be too early in the day for most of them. Having checked my master wasn't in, I took a table as far away from the nearest occupied one as I could. My talk with Edwin would best be kept away from ears which shouldn't hear it. Whelan, the owner, came over and looked me up and down before asking for my order. Not being used to such places I stuttered a reply.

'I'm waiting on a friend ... Mr Hare ... I expect you know him. He'll be here soon.'

Whelan grunted and walked away. The room was quieter and better furnished than taverns I had been in, and the air smelled a damned sight better, though not an aroma I recognised. At each table, two or three men, smoking pipes, talked, pausing from time to time to sip from their cups. Most appeared to be enjoying the drink, though I did see one man screw up his nose as if only taking it to stay in good company.

Edwin arrived a couple of minutes after we'd agreed and ordered two drinks, before placing a small cloth bag on the table. He waved me to open it. Inside were as many coins as I'd earn in a week as a gardener.

'No, Edwin, it's too much.'

'It is nothing, only what you deserve, you carried out your tasks well, and it is only a fraction of what I have been offered for my services. I have yet to be paid but I can spare enough to pay you, which I would rather do in case I need to leave Bridgnorth.'

'You're going away?'

'I do not want to but may be forced if I do not find

Steps' killer.'

'That might be difficult.'

'It may, the man had many victims who would be glad he is dead.'

'That's not quite what I meant, Edwin.'

'What then?'

I gritted my teeth. 'They're saying you did it.'

Annoyance flashed in Edwin's eyes. 'Is that what you think, Meg Valentine? If it is, you can go and be damned like the rest of them.'

'How can I be sure? Look at it from my position. You ask me to follow Steps and find where he lives. You ask me to enquire of those ... those thieves ... if he had sold anything to them. And you went to his home.'

Now the eyes narrowed. 'How do you know this?'

I drew a deep breath. There was no going back now. 'Because I saw you there.'

'When? How?'

'I was practising the skills we talked about and wanted to know if I'd improved enough to follow without you noticing. I watched you leave your house and stayed well back through all the streets and lanes. If you'd seen me, I had an excuse ready, but you didn't, and I managed to keep you in sight until you reached Cartway. Then I guessed where you were heading. Once you'd gone down the hill, and I saw you knock his door, I went home, happy I'd succeeded. It can't have been more than half an hour before Steps was found dead.'

'You know, when we first met, Meg, I could tell

there was something about you would make you fit this job, and now you have proved it. Well done.'

'You're not angry?'

'Part of me is. I do not take kindly to being spied upon then accused of murder, but most of me is impressed. You have shown the initiative to keep working hard at developing your craft, and you have shown you are not afraid to tackle a suspected villain head on.'

I didn't now know what to think. He'd flattered me but not denied killing Ben Steps. So, I could back away and bury my suspicions, or I could chance a further question. Would he still be "impressed" if I wasn't deterred? 'I'm sorry, Edwin, but you've not really explained why your accusers are wrong.'

'Then I'm afraid you will have to take me on trust because I cannot prove I am innocent. Indeed, the story I would tell you to explain my interest in Steps may only shore up any doubts you have. If it does, then ask yourself why I would tell it.'

'If you want me to take you on trust then you've got to do the same for me and tell me your tale. I can then make my own mind up if I believe you or no.'

Edwin looked over to catch Whelan's attention and raised two fingers in the air. I shook my head violently. I'd be sick if I drank another drop of the foul liquid dispensed in the place.

He lowered one finger and grinned. 'So be it, coffee is not to everyone's taste, and I have no desire to spend good money on something destined for the slop bucket. God knows it is expensive enough.'

We waited for Whelan to return with Edwin's drink before he continued. 'I need to go back many years' Meg, to a time when I was much younger even than you.' He stopped and grabbed my wrist. 'I can trust you with this? You must not say a word to anyone.'

'I won't say anything.'

'Good. I grew up far from here, in Cumberland, on the border with Scotland. Terrible things happened to my parents, and I embarked on a life which put me outside the law of this land for a time. I'll tell you no more of that now but suffice to say Steps somehow discovered this and demanded money to keep it quiet. I know I was not the only one he tried to pressure for money, using past secrets against them. He sent me notes but did not reveal his identity, which is why I asked you to follow him. I went to see him, and he was not there, so I asked questions of his neighbours, a foolish thing to have done.

'I went back later, which is when you followed me, just to find the lie of the land and decide what I should do. His door was slightly open when I arrived, so I pushed it and went inside. Steps was dead, his throat cut. I knew how this might look if I reported it, so I took a few minutes to search for his evidence, and for the items he had stolen from your mistress. I found only some of hers and nothing of mine.'

'And you just left him there, Edwin?'

'What else could I do? There was no help for him, and it would only cause me trouble. Which it has. The man was evil and deserved what he got, but I swear I did not kill him.'

Despite myself, I couldn't help feeling these might just be words, but there was little point in pressing him further.

'I'll believe you. For now. But I think the best thing we can do is find out who actually murdered Steps. If it wasn't you.'

At the sound of her husband's voice, Sarah quickened her pace across the hall, until the click of his door stopped her in her tracks. She turned to face him, a smile displayed for his benefit.

'Aubrey. You called?'

The magistrate crooked a finger, as he often did on the bench when drawing a defendant in for the judicial advice he was about to administer. 'A word, my dear.'

'But I was just going -'

'Now, please. Come in and take a seat. This will not take long.'

Sarah ducked under his arm as he held open the door and made her way to an armchair by the window.

Aubrey stopped her. 'No, no, here, by the desk.'

She now knew she was to be treated to one of his master-servant admonitions, and which role she would be expected to play.

The bills spread across his desk hinted at what may have caused Aubrey's displeasure. He sat across from her and placed his hands, palms down and fingers splayed, on the papers. 'I see you have worked out why I wish to speak to you, Sarah. This cannot go on.'

Aubrey lifted a sheet and wafted it in front of Sarah's face. 'Two bonnets. Not one, but two. On top of the two you ordered last month.' He put down the bill and picked up another. 'And here, a pair of high leather boots.'

Sarah lowered her eyes. 'They are things I needed, Aubrey.'

'Needed? Or wanted? No-one needs four bonnets, nor several pairs of boots.' He waved his hands across the entire desk. 'And what about the rest? Did you "need" a new dress ... or two petticoats ... or -' He slammed down a fist. 'I despair of this kind of behaviour, Sarah. It is not what I want in my wife.'

'Do you not wish me to look pretty for you, Aubrey?'

He laughed. 'I might not object to your spending if I thought it was for me.'

'Of course it is for you.'

'You must not take me for a fool, Sarah.'

'What do you mean? You know there is no-one but you.'

Aubrey stood and leant across the desk. 'Do you think I am not aware you despise me? Why would a handsome woman such as yourself want to be tied to an older man like me. If your father had not been so indebted he would surely have hung on to you until a fine young farmer or tradesman came along to sweep you off your feet. Where would you be then, I wonder. A little wife with a carpenter as a husband and six or eight hungry children crying in the corner of your cottage. Instead,' he swept his arm around the room, 'you have all this. A fine house, grand gardens, servants. Yet still you flutter your eyes at men and let them kiss you.'

Sarah sat back in her chair, the fire now in her cheeks. She glared at her husband.

'What? You accuse me of this? When did I do such a thing?'

'I saw you with Josh Jenkins.'

'Pfft. That horrid man followed me around from the moment he and his equally horrid wife arrived. He sniffed and dribbled like a dog the whole time. The only reason I did not slap his face when he kissed me was because he is your friend. I had hoped, vainly it turned out, you would pull him off and throw him from the house. You did not, preferring to keep a customer happy than rescue your wife's honour. In fact, I believe you enjoyed watching him pawing at me.'

'Honour? You talk of honour? It does not escape my attention the way men look at you when we are about. Sometimes I even see their admiring glances returned.'

'Aubrey, you are mistaken. Show me proof. You can't, can you?'

Her husband walked round the desk and placed his hands on her shoulders. Sarah stiffened as they slid sideways, and his fingers curled around her throat.

'If I had proof, you would no longer be my wife. You would be out on the streets. Penniless. I would soon have another. Someone to warm my bed and to look after our child.'

Sarah gasped. 'You would be so heartless as to take Hannah from me?'

'Believe that I would, in an instant. Why would I punish a poor child for her mother's indiscretion? The girl is mine and deserves to share in my good fortune. She would most probably starve if I threw her out with you.'

Aubrey released his grip on Sarah's throat, then leant forward and kissed the top of her head. 'Now take yourself back to your room, my dear, and remember my words. Remember them very well.'

I left Edwin to his coffee and his thoughts and made my way back towards home, taking a diversion around St Leonard's to gather my thoughts. At least if my master or mistress saw me I could say I'd been looking to see if any work was required.

Though I thought it unlikely Edwin was Steps' killer, he'd admitted to being a lawbreaker in the past. If his sins were so great to have left him open to extortion, then he might have it in him to silence anyone who threatened his good name. What would have been so bad that Steps thought he could profit from it?

Could Edwin have killed someone when he was young, and run south to Shropshire to avoid capture?

Something he'd said nibbled away in my head until I reached the quiet of the churchyard, then it struck me. Edwin had mentioned Scotland. Could he be a Jacobite? As a supporter of the Catholic Stuarts his livelihood at least would be under threat if it came out. If he'd fought on their side in the rebellion a few years' back it might even put his liberty in danger. Certainly something he'd want to be kept quiet. But would he be willing to kill to ensure it was?

He'd only given me part of the story, the part shared by several victims, Steps was trying to extort money from him. I couldn't decide if his explanation of finding Steps' body then calmly going through his belongings rang true. Would I do such a thing? I don't think so. I'd run a mile.

Then there was the question of paying me. Had he only mentioned this after I told him I'd followed him? Was it an attempt to keep me quiet? For the life of me I couldn't remember when it first came up.

Edwin had admitted my mistress hadn't paid him, so why was he so keen to settle his debt? I certainly wasn't pressing him. In fact, I didn't expect to receive any payment for my time, grateful only for his help to escape my current life.

Two circuits round the churchyard and I was no clearer in my head about Edwin's innocence or guilt, though I could spend no more time away from my duties.

As the lane at the side of Cliffe House came into view, I saw my mistress walking quickly from it. Fortunately, she didn't look in my direction and turned towards the town. I only glimpsed her face for a second, and even this was at a distance, but her cheeks glistened as if wet. Had she been crying?

Sixteen

Edwin wondered if his explanation to Meg had been enough. The last thing he needed was the girl poking around his past. Steps had been disposed of, but this didn't mean he could chance letting down his guard. Meg seemed a decent enough character, but experience had told Edwin his trust should not be given lightly.

Soon after leaving Meg, he turned into West Castle Street, only to be pulled up short by his name being called by Sarah. 'Mr Hare. It is you is it not? Could you kindly spare me a moment '

He quickened his step, wishing to avoid contact with the woman who had thrown him into such confusion at their last meeting. His attraction to her quickly arrested his departure. After all, he had not been repulsed by her offer, only surprised, not knowing how to react. He lifted his hat and bowed stiffly before responding in the public style they had adopted. 'Madam. I did not expect to see you again so soon. Nothing is amiss, I hope. You appear a little agitated.'

Sarah took a deep breathed and spread her hands, palm forward, in front of her.

'All is well, sir. May I walk alongside you?'

'Of course.'

Sarah leaned in towards Edwin, lowering her voice. 'I must apologise, sir.'

'There is no need.'

'I cannot imagine what you must think of me. All I can say in my defence is that I have been under much pressure since my letters were stolen. Quite out of my mind with worry about what will happen if my husband discovers their existence.' Sarah looked away. 'I am so sorry for the embarrassment I have caused you.'

'As I have said, madam, think nothing of it. Now, is there anything further?'

'You are still angry with me; what can I say to make you less so?'

'You do not need to say anything, Mrs Beaumont. I was simply a little surprised at your... proposition... but I will put it to one side, and you will go home to your good husband.'

'Good?' the words were almost spat. 'Husband he maybe, but good he is not. I would never have offered to cuckold him if my marriage was a happy one.'

Sarah turned her face to the wall, and Edwin saw her shoulders shaking. He wanted to pull her to him, but knew if he did, this would be the end of the pair of them in the town. Instead, he moved to shield her distress from passers-by, making as if to look at an item of interest in a shop window. It did not take long for his companion to recover her composure to the point where she could commence her conversation once again. They walked on as if nothing had happened.

'You work for my husband, Mr Hare, but you do not know him as I do. He is a cruel, vindictive man and I only agreed to the marriage to save my father from ruin. I had hoped he may change once we set up home together, but he did not. If Aubrey had the slightest inkling of my past friendship with Owen Ambrose, he would throw me out and cut me off without a farthing. Even worse, he's told me he would keep Hannah and never let her see me again if such a thing happened.'

'And if he knew we were meeting in secret?'

Sarah stopped her progress.

'Is that what we are doing, Mr Hare?'

'I think so, don't you? We go through this charade of bumping into one another, then exchange whispers until we part. However, this is unimportant. You engaged me to do a job for you, I did it. You cannot pay and I must put it down to experience. So, you go home, keep your secrets, and we will not meet again.'

Edwin bowed to take his leave. As he turned away, Sarah touched him on the forearm. 'But what if I wish to meet?'

Edwin swallowed hard and glanced up and down the street. 'I've told you already, Mrs Beaumont, I don't want repayment in that manner.'

'It would not be repayment. It would be because I wanted to.'

Edwin closed his eyes and rubbed his forehead.

'Then we would have to see what may be arranged. Now, it is perhaps better that I leave you to your shopping.'

He stepped away and bowed once more.

'Before you go, Mr Hare, a final word. I *will* find a way to repay you.'

Edwin left Sarah, his mind spinning from their conversation. He was not exactly unused to being propositioned by women, but not often by ones of Sarah Beaumont's station. Gabriella Luca was an exception, but he suspected she thought of him like some exotic creation, so far beneath her as to be an object of fascination. Like the fruit her gardener grew in the orangery behind her home. The magistrate's wife did not seem to him someone to be taken with such whims.

A woman's voice disturbed his thoughts, and he turned to see one of advancing years, leaning on a stick. 'Mr Hare, is it?'

'It is.'

'I hear that you have been accused of that man's killing.'

Edwin nodded. 'You know of this?'

'Everyone in the town knows. I, for one, do not believe it. You performed a service for my cousin, and she has nothing but praise for you.'

'That is most kind of you to say, Madam.'

She gestured towards the other end of town where Cartway ran down the hill. 'Just because you were seen there, it does not mean you had anything to do with that evil man's death. Will you walk with me for a while?'

Edwin agreed that he would, and she passed him a basket containing vegetables from the market. He smiled and nodded, then offered his arm for support, which the woman accepted. They made their way along High Street, with her shaking her head and complaining of the prices in the shop windows, until they turned left and began to descend the hill.

'He was visited by many folk, Mr Hare. Rich and poor, it could have been any of them. Why, even the magistrate's fine wife was there, and no one is accusing her, are they?'

'You mean Mrs Beaumont? She visited Steps?'

'She did. Not more than an hour before you. Tried to hide her face, but I would know that young woman anywhere. I used to work for her family. I left them a few months after she married. She did not see me.'

They reached Steps' cottage, and the woman pointed over her shoulder to a house across the lane. 'I live there, and I'd not miss much down this part of the town. Half the people in Bridgnorth pass by at some time.'

Edwin smiled. Although he did not approve of busybodies filling their dull days with the lives of other people, he knew his job would be so much more difficult without them. 'And you have told the magistrate of this?'

She spat on the ground.

'Why would I do such a thing? Ben Steps deserved

to die, and I am not sorry to see him gone. If Mrs Beaumont was the one who did for him, then good luck to her. She has served the whole town a favour. The lady was only ever kind to me, and I wish her no harm. Neither do I wish you come to harm, which is why I tell you what I have seen. Make of it as you will, and use it as you must.'

With this she scurried over to the house she had pointed to, disappearing inside the door, and leaving Edwin perplexed.

He knew he would have little chance of catching Sarah before she reached her home, and he could not wait to speak to her until his next visit to her husband in the afternoon. The information Steps' neighbour had given provided an excuse for him to attend the magistrate again, though Edwin knew it would be a serious risk if Beaumont saw him speaking to Sarah.

Joseph answered the door and Edwin asked to speak to his master.

'I am afraid Mr Beaumont is not at home, sir, he left on business a short time ago.'

'And will he be back soon?'

'I can't say, the master informed me he would be a couple of hours, but he may be longer.'

'In that case, would you ask Mrs Beaumont if I may have a word?'

Joseph frowned. '*Mrs* Beaumont?'

'I need to leave a confidential message to be passed to the magistrate, as soon as he returns.'

'Then you may tell me.'

'As I said, it is confidential, man, not for your ears to be spread around every tavern in Bridgnorth. Now, tell your mistress I would speak to her, or Mr Beaumont will hear of it.'

Five minutes later, Edwin had been led through to the garden by Joseph and told to wait whilst Mrs Beaumont readied herself to meet with him. He could feel the eyes of the household on him, though could see no-one at the windows.

When Sarah came out, the footman watched for a moment from the doorway, until she turned and told him to go back inside. He paused for a second and clearly decided he should do as he had been told.

Sarah gestured for Edwin to follow her and took him to a seat surrounded by shrubs, completely shielded from any prying eyes in the house. 'Please sit, Mr Hare. I imagine what you have to say may take more than a minute or two. Especially if you are prepared to put both of our reputations in jeopardy.'

'For this I can only apologise, Mrs Beaumont, but I have been given information which requires me to speak with you.'

'What information might this be?'

'You were seen leaving Ben Steps home at about the time he died.'

Sarah gasped and stood, clasping a hand to her mouth.

'Who would say such a thing?'

'It does not matter who told me, but is it true?'

She lowered herself slowly back to her seat, her

knuckles white from grasping the arm. 'There would appear to be no point in denying it, but it means nothing, Steps was alive when I left him.'

'Will you tell me what took place between you?'

'You will not use it against me?'

Edwin shook his head. 'If you say you are innocent of any wrongdoing then I shall believe you and it need go no further. If I sense you are being untruthful, or not telling me the complete story, I will need to consider what I do. So, please, hold nothing back.'

Sarah looked down and stroked the folds of her dress, clearly gathering her thoughts. 'I had sent my footman to pay the ransom fee and to recover my letters, but Steps took the money then refused to return them. This stretched me to my wits' end, and it is true, I resolved to take them back by physical threat. I am not a violent woman, not by any means, but I could see no alternative. So, I took with me a knife. At first, I had the simple intention of threatening Steps when he let me in, but as I got closer to his cottage my anger grew and grew. I think I would have stuck the dagger in his throat, had this stayed with me but the man could see I had not the courage to use it. He laughed in my face. He was still laughing when I ran from his door.'

'You are saying you did not kill him? Despite the damage he could cause you?'

'I did not. When I heard he had been murdered I wished I *had* done it. The vengeance would have been so sweet, but it was not to be.'

'The difficulty I have with your story, madam, is

Steps was not an imposing man. He was small. A weasel. And a woman of your age and virility would overpower him easily. Someone killed the man, and you have admitted you went to see him with that intention.'

'But I did not go through with it. I held the knife to his throat and that is all. You may believe me or believe me not. I have nothing further I can say to prove my innocence.' She glared at Edwin. 'But I *am* innocent.'

Edwin stared at Sarah for a long moment, trying to discern if she was lying, then made his conclusion.

'Then you cannot be punished for the mere thought. If you could, we would all be in trouble.'

It surprised me to hear voices in the garden, especially those voices.

Dad had told me to tidy a corner where the rosebay had become so big it didn't flower much any more. We'd little knowledge of this shrub. It had grown a lot over the past two years, and my father hoped a sharp pruning might help. I'd completed the cutting back and begun to clear the debris when I heard my mistress and a man talking. It took me a moment to recognise Edwin's voice, but his accent told me it was him, even before I peeked through the greenery to see the pair seated on the bench. I ducked, praying neither had seen nor heard me, and held my breath until I feared my lungs would burst.

The half-expected reprimand did not come, so I

leant back and listened. I was too far away to hear any conversation, other than when my mistress, clearly displeased, raised her voice. I knew if I was ever to make any progress as a thief-taker I must learn to observe from a distance without being observed myself. So, I shifted to my knees and, keeping my head where I hoped I couldn't be seen, spied on the couple as best I could.

Mrs Beaumont was standing, her face most agitated. When Edwin spoke, she seemed to sink onto her seat as if unwell, and I wondered if I should own up to being there and to offer help, but only seconds passed before she recovered. Their discussion began again, with my mistress speaking at some length, with much gesturing, as though explaining something to Edwin. When she'd finished, he remained silent for a short while, then his features softened and spoke so gently not a sound reached me, but she smiled in response.

If I'd been confused by seeing them speaking secretly together, it didn't compare to the shock I felt when they finished speaking and stood. Not a word passed between them when my mistress took Edwin's hand. Nor when he pulled her to him in an embrace. It was only a moment before she pushed him away, but this seemed a moment too long.

Outside Ben Steps' cottage a man was piling furniture, all of poor quality, onto a barrow. The remains of the dead man's life. I stood back when Edwin approached him. 'Good evening, sir, would you mind if we had a look through these?'

'Tis of no concern of mine, I've been asked by the landlord to clear the place and make it ready for his next tenant.'

The labourer moved away and leant against the wall. He lit his pipe and watched the smoke curl upwards in the still air.

We lifted a chest from the pile and laid it on the ground. Edwin pulled open each drawer in turn and rifled through its contents. There appeared to be nothing of interest until he reached the third drawer, where a bible lay. He flipped through the pages, and two sheets of paper dropped out. Edwin read them, then passed them to me. 'You are able to read, Meg?'

'Of course.'

Despite my brave reply I didn't read well. My dad taught me my letters so I could help him in the garden. Plant names I recognise well enough, and can usually work out messages if the words aren't too long, but that's as far as it goes.

The first page held ten names in two columns, one of eight and one of two. Most had only a last name and an initial. Two obvious ones were E Hare and S Beaumont, which most likely were Edwin and my mistress. Another I recognised was that of J Crowe, almost certainly Joseph. His name was next to Mrs Beaumont's. One, W Downes, could possibly be my master's cousin Mr Walter Downes. Though I knew people with the remaining names, Weale, Norris, Trussle, Roden and Allen, they were common enough and their initials didn't help. At the side of Edwin's was written another, Quentin Goode. This name, and an address, was also on a second sheet, in the same untidy hand as the rest. I handed the papers back to Edwin.

'Could these be Steps' victims?'

He ran his finger down the list twice.

'I would think so, though some might be Steps' informants. I could make a good stab at who some of them are. Weale is possibly our local member of parliament. Most of those are corrupt in my opinion, so Steps may have discovered something which might make this one a target. I've heard the name Norris recently, and I cannot think where, but it will come to me. There's an Indigo Trussle helps out in the courts, so he's a possibility. I have to admit the names Roden and Allen have me foxed. You have seen your mistress's name is here, as is mine, and Mr Downes. I imagine that footman of hers gave Steps the information which put her in his power.'

I shook my head. 'I can't see it. When I spoke to Joseph, he claimed he didn't know this man was in Bridgnorth until he went to see him on my mistress's behalf.'

'Then I will need to talk to him myself.'

I grabbed a battered shoe from the pile of rubbish and threw it at the cottage wall. 'You don't trust my judgment then?'

'Calm yourself, Meg. I've met many liars in my life. More than you have, I would imagine. I have come to appreciate how good some of them are. Your Joseph may be one of them, that is all, and it would be better for me to hear his story too. Just in case. Believe me, I will not be checking your work all the time. If I did, there would be little point in me having you as an "apprentice," would there?' He turned his attention to the second sheet. 'See what we have here? This man, Goode, written next to me. I think we must go and find him tomorrow.'

'Could he have had something to do with Steps' death?'

'Not necessarily, though I would have them all as suspects at the minute. His is the only one with an address, so will be a good place to start. I have no idea why Steps would associate me with this person.'

Seventeen

There used to be a window in the space above my bed, or so I'm told. Even before my dad was born it had been closed up to save on the window tax. All that remains is a hole about the size of four bricks, to allow air into my small room. For the winter months I keep it stuffed with rags to keep out the cold, but from spring to autumn I take them out, giving me some ease from the horse smells below. It also pleases me stand on a stool and spy down on the front garden. The view I get is small, only a narrow section which includes part of the path, the gate, and a sliver of the lane beyond. Even this is only possible by standing on tiptoe or crouching. It's not much but is enough to keep an eye on the comings and goings to the house, or to watch my father carrying out his inspections of the garden.

This morning I'd got up at first light, as I usually do, and completed my early jobs of feeding and grooming the horses, then turning the compost heaps once I'd thrown the night's manure on to them. I returned to my room and, whilst I took a mug of small beer, I looked out from my peep-hole to see thrushes and blackbirds pecking for their breakfast. I heard no sound to frighten them but, without warning, they all flew away. I thought perhaps a cat or even a fox had crept too close, and I moved position to try to catch a glimpse. Instead of some prowling animal, my mistress came into view, walking in the direction of the gate. Seconds later she stepped through and turned left towards the town.

Before I could give any further thought to where she might be going, I spotted another movement on the lane. It was Edwin and he seemed to have been hiding, waiting for Mrs Beaumont to leave, for he followed her a moment later.

I jumped from my bed and ran headlong down the stairs, praying I wouldn't lose them by taking the long way through the side gate. I'd no choice about going that way because I'd surely be dismissed if my employer saw me using the front entrance. As I heard my father's voice call from the side garden, I cursed and wished I'd taken the chance to go the other way.

'Meg, where are you off this time of day?'

I stopped my dash and turned to face my dad.

'Nowhere.'

He grunted. 'Seem to be trying to get nowhere in a hurry.'

'Sorry. I just hoped to make it to the market and back before you needed me.'

'Well you won't. I need you now.'

Much as I love my father and my work, this was one of the times I wished I could be free of them both.

Edwin glanced up at Cliffe House when he saw its mistress come out from the gate. As far as he could tell, no-one watched from the windows. The magistrate's room lay at the back, as did the kitchen and the nursery. Beaumont would be busy, and it would be unlikely any servants would need to be at the front of the house at this time of day.

He waited until Sarah passed the Grammar School corner before setting off after her. She had not left at any speed, and it took no effort to reach the corner himself in time to see her turn into Moat Lane, the short street leading to the Northgate. He didn't continue directly after her but took a narrow passageway to the left. He strode on until taking another on the right to bring him on to High Street, ahead of Sarah.

She was not immediately in sight, but then Edwin saw her leave a shop on the opposite side of the street. He walked across to meet her, as if he had walked up from his home.

Sarah stopped when she saw him and glanced round to see if anyone in the vicinity might know her. She erred on the side of caution. 'Why Mr Hare, an unexpected pleasure to see you again.'

Edwin grinned and tipped his hat brim. 'And you, Mrs Beaumont. Might I walk with you for a stretch? I have a favour to ask of you and your good husband.'

Without waiting for confirmation, he fell in by Sarah's side. She leant in towards him and whispered.

'What is this about, Edwin? I do not believe you met me here by chance.'

'I needed to see you. After yesterday.'

'You must do it more carefully. I cannot afford for us to be seen walking together in the town so often.'

'If not here, then where?'

'I often stroll by the river. We could meet there with less chance of being seen by anyone who might relay information back to Aubrey. As long as we avoid the area near his boatyard, we should be able to remain discrete.'

'When will you go again?'

'Aubrey is away tomorrow, so it will be easy to slip out in the morning with no questions asked.'

Before Edwin could reply, Sarah straightened and took the merest step sideways, to put a respectable distance between them once more. She raised a hand in greeting to an elegantly dressed woman, some years older than herself. They exchanged a few words about the weather and the woman went on her way. Edwin suspected she may have taken a glance back over her shoulder. She could not have failed to notice how closely he and Sarah were in conversation.

'You see, Edwin, meeting that lady could have been disastrous. Fortunately, I know her not to be a gossip, and she would have no dealings with my husband, so no finger will be pointed on this occasion.

'Now, what was the favour you required? There is no doubt I am in your debt.'

'I want the assistance of your young gardener, Meg Valentine, for a few hours. She has helped me in her spare time, but I need a little more. The girl has the skill and sensitivity to make something of herself and has proved useful to me. By turns, this has also been useful to you and your husband. If Meg can be allowed a little more freedom, she may also help me clear my name.'

Sarah paused for a moment before answering. 'Then I must agree. I am deeply aware I have not settled my debt to you so I will endeavour to explain Meg's absence away to my husband if he notices. You must speak to him yourself and gain his permission properly if you need her again. Now, we must part before tongues begin to wag.'

She turned and walked away a few paces before turning back. 'I will see you tomorrow ... Edwin.'

I had agreed to meet Edwin at Quentin Goode's house and had to rush the job Dad had given me. Even so, I was late for our agreed time and found Edwin waiting outside a fine brick building on Underhill. Though I wanted to ask why he had been outside Cliffe House so early, I thought better of it. He knocked and a maid took us through to a room with a view of the river, not thirty paces away.

A man, with a face as creased as any I had ever seen, sat in an armchair by a roaring fire. I ran a finger inside my collar to ease the heat and was glad I worked in the open air. Edwin introduced us, and explained that we had found his name, alongside others, on papers left by the dead Ben Steps

'Are you sure you want to talk with this girl here?' Quentin Goode raised a bony finger in my direction. 'There may be things you prefer her not to know.'

Edwin glanced at me then back at the old man slumped in his chair. 'In what way?'

Goode cackled, which brought on such a fit of coughing and wheezing I thought we would need to fetch help. When it subsided, spittle dribbled from his lips as he spoke. 'You have come to me with a story that you have found my name next to yours on a list discovered at a dead man's home. I imagine you suspect the other names are those of his victims. How could there not be secrets tied up in this? If there are things you wish to keep quiet, why would you want her,' the finger pointed again, 'to hear them?'

Edwin rubbed his chin. 'You might be right,' He turned to me. 'Would you leave us for a while, Meg.'

'But Edwin -'

'Do not argue. If we are to work together you must learn there are times when you may be present, and times when you may not. This is one of the latter.'

I crossed my arms and planted my feet firmly.

'Meg.' Edwin raised his voice only slightly above its normal level, enough to let me know he was serious. 'Away. I will not ask again. If my talk with Mr Goode here reveals anything of relevance, be sure I will tell you. Be also sure it will not always be this way. Please allow me a little freedom on this occasion.'

His mix of authority and pleading left me no choice but to make my exit, unsure if what they were to discuss might incriminate Edwin in Steps' death. I could see I may need to begin my own enquiries on that front.

Edwin watched from Goode's door until he was sure Meg had gone, still unsure if he should have sent her away. He knew if he wanted to convince the girl he was innocent he would need to tell her something close to the truth, but he would rather have it under his control. Better than through the ramblings of a sick old man.

It was easy to see Goode would not be much longer in this world and would have nothing to lose regardless of what he might reveal. Edwin pulled a chair from the side of the room and sat at Goode's table. 'I should explain, Mr Goode, there were several names on that list, and I *do* suspect most were victims of Steps' attempts to extort money. I was one of them, though he was killed before he could wring anything from me. Your name was next to mine, as though we had some association. I don't believe we've ever met. Am I correct?'

'You are, sir, though I know something of your past.'

Edwin clenched and unclenched his fists, waiting for a moment before asking his question. 'Could you tell me how you know Ben Steps?'

Goode coughed again, not fiercely, but enough to create an uncomfortable pause before he replied, his voice hoarse as a bullfrog's. The man gasped after each phrase. 'I worked for his father for years. I did not know him as Steps then. It was Burney.'

Edwin drew a breath. He had not heard that name for a while, and the memory of it was not pleasant. Now he understood the connection.

Quentin Goode paused, as if waiting for the information to sink in. 'You recognise it, Mr Hare? From his brother? The one you murdered?'

'I did not murder him.'

'The man died at your hand. An honourable and decent man. Worth a hundred of the one calling himself Steps.'

'If that is what you think of Steps then why betray me to him?'

'It was never my intention to do so. We met one day in a tavern and got to talking. At first, I thought him to be a stranger, but as the ale went down, I realised he was his father's son. I had heard his assumed name around the town and knew him not to be any kind of decent fellow. One with many enemies by all accounts. He and his father, Sir Edward, had parted company when Ben was barely fifteen years. Before my time. Sir Edward rarely spoke of him, good or ill. I respected my old employer, I moved from my home in Whitchurch to join him on his estate near Upton Magna, and he always treated me well. I felt a loyalty to him and his family. He took his own life a year after Kevin Burney, the older brother, was slain.'

Edwin shook his head. 'I still do not understand. I can see you owed Sir Edward a debt, but why make me the price to settle it?'

'It was not something I did with intent. Steps and I

talked and drank, sharing tales of his old home. After a while we passed out until the innkeeper roused us, then we drank some more. Steps began to weep for his dead father and his dead brother, and so I told him I knew what had happened and who had killed him. I did not know he would use it against you.'

I waited across the street for Edwin to finish his talk with Quentin Goode. I fumed for the first while, then calmed as the sun fell on my face, and I wondered how I might encourage Edwin to tell me his story. The sounds of men on the bridge bounced along the river. They shouted down to those on the trows as they threw ropes to haul the boats upstream, and there was much cursing and laughter. The splashing of the great wheel, pumping water up to High Town, gave a rhythm to the scene and made me think what a hive of activity the riverside was, providing wealth to my master and the townsmen like him.

High on the hill above, the bell of Saint Mary Magdalene's rang the quarter hour and Edwin pushed out into the light.

He raised a hand without a smile when he saw me. 'You are still here, Meg?'

'Did you think I'd just leave with no explanation from you? I'm not your servant, Edwin, to be dismissed at your whim.'

The black cloud across his face blew away and he grinned. 'My, you are a gritty young woman, full of fire and bile. If you were a boy I'd be tempted to box your ears for your impudence.'

'I'd like to see you try, girl or no. But come on, I don't want to argue. I can see your talk with that man, Goode, has bothered you. Won't you tell me what's going on?'

He thought for a moment then crooked a finger. 'Let's walk along the river and I will tell as much as I can, but you must promise not to reveal it to another living soul.'

I nodded and he continued.

'I told you before that I come from the north of this country. The shire of Cumberland. Do you know of it?'

'Only by name.'

'It is a fine county, with a wild coast and wilder countryside. My father said his family had lived on that land for centuries, though my mother came from over the border. They always practised the old religion even in the outlawed times.'

'You are a Papist, Edwin?'

'Let us admit that my parents were, and they taught me their ways in my childhood.'

'You said before that something bad happened to them. What was it?'

He stopped and stared into the water flowing fast beyond the bank. 'It began when I was a few years younger than you are now. I helped my father eke out an existence on barren moors. We had not much but what we had was our own and won with our hard labour. It was enough to feed us and to pay our rent to a lord who would spend as much on a single entertainment as we would receive in a year. Then the soldiers came.

'I know not what was said but saw them from a distance. I watched as they stabbed my father with their bayonets and took my mother inside.' Edwin picked up a stone and threw it into the river, the ripples spreading quickly in all directions. 'To my eternal shame I did nothing but hide. Later I was told they were clearing a way for a road through his lordship's land to make easier travel northwards for King George's troops. It seems they were ordering my father to quit, and he argued, so they disposed of the problem.'

'God's teeth. But I don't see how this would make you prey to Steps.'

'It was what happened later. When the soldiers had gone, I found my parents and my young sister dead. I ran and I hid for two days, looking for Father Gregory, a priest sheltered in a neighbouring estate, who gave us the sacraments from time to time. He arranged for his benefactor to give me work and a roof. Once a week he would call me to him and talk of ways I might find revenge. After two years, he told me I must accompany some men loyal to the true king, James, travelling to northern towns to whip up riots against George.'

'That's treason, Edwin.'

'It can only be treason if the king on the throne is legitimate. This one isn't. I continued for a few years more. Up and down the country I would travel, soon leading a band of my own men. We would spread amongst the working places and the taverns, passing on gossip and stories of how George and his court lived in luxury whilst we were subject to every tax under the sun. We also told the tale, at every opportunity, that the King Across the Water would soon return and we must be ready. In forty-five he did.'

'Was that the end of it?'

'Hardly, just the beginning. All of us engaged in this joined the forces supporting Prince Charles Edward Stuart. For my part, I fell in with Francis Towneley and his Manchester Regiment, and I fought in skirmishes until we took Carlisle in November of that year. We held the town only a few weeks when The Duke of Cumberland's men overran it. We faced cannon fire for days, then fought in the streets. Many had surrendered. I was about to do the same when a soldier cornered me. He made to kill me but, me being bigger, stronger and more battle hardened, I relieved him of his weapon. For what seemed like an age, he looked bewildered when his musket rattled across the ground. Then, with a fearsome cry, he ran towards me and impaled himself on my bayonet. As he lay dying, blood oozing from his lips, he gave me his name and begged me to let his father know he had died bravely. The poor lad was barely whiskered.'

'And did you do so?'

'I had no chance. Knowing I'd now be executed if captured, I fled Carlisle at nightfall and made my escape southwards. I could see the Prince's fortunes were turning, with much discontent amongst his followers. The whole episode sickened me to the point

I no longer wanted truck with fights between kings where good men, and boys like Kevin Burney, would die.'

'I still don't understand the connection to Steps.'

'Kevin Burney was his brother.'

The shock of this made me gasp. 'So he wanted revenge.'

'The rat didn't hold such high principles. When he heard from Quentin Goode that the man, a Jacobite and a Catholic, who had killed his brother lived nearby, Steps saw an opportunity to grasp more money to his bosom. True, when we met, he offered me a choice, pay up or give myself up, but I am certain it was the cash he wanted. Goode tells me he and Steps had been drinking heavily when he revealed information about my past and he meant me no harm.'

Though I knew Edwin may have a reason to see Steps' dead, I'd not expected it to be so serious. There was now no doubt in my mind he would be a suspect if anyone else was looking into the man's murder. After all, it'd be revealed another man had died at his hand. Could his questioning of others simply be laying a false scent?

'Have you told my master, all this?'

'Why would I? As far as he is aware I arrived here three years' ago, and my past is my own business. I would not wish to spoil that illusion. After I left Carlisle, I heard that Charles Stuart was heading back to Scotland, so I travelled the opposite way. I spent two months working my way southwards before arriving in Bridgnorth to a new occupation. I had heard that Mr Beaumont had need of a man with an eye to find villains and I saw no reason why I could not do so. If it had not been for Steps, I could have lived a long and peaceful life in this town.'

'So will you leave?'

'Not yet. If I cannot find someone for the magistrate I may have to make a run for it, though do not wish to spend the rest of my days as a fugitive. I have done enough of that already in my life. In case I do need to go, could I ask a favour?'

I shrugged.

'I will take that as a "yes." I wish to meet with Mrs Beaumont again. Could you pass a message?'

Edwin appeared so wretched in his predicament; I could hardly refuse. If he proved innocent of Steps' killing, then I'd need to stay in his good books. I'd also need to ensure my master didn't find I was helping his rival.

Eighteen

Edwin parted from Meg unsure if he had done the right thing in revealing his secrets. For so long he had kept his past to himself, fearful of confiding in anyone. Yet now he felt strangely elated, a burden shared. He also shook with the thought he was now more vulnerable than he had been an hour earlier and could not imagine how he had been led to tell all to the girl. One thing he did know was she would go far in her chosen line of work if she could extract secrets quite so easily.

They had separated at her gate, with Edwin adding a second request, for her to ask Joseph to join him in the lane as soon as he could.

Within moments the footman was there. 'You wished to see me Mr Hare? Is it about that man Steps again?'

'Indeed it is.'

'Well I told you all I know last time we spoke.'

'But the situation has changed now, Joseph, has it not?' Steps is now dead and cold, with his throat cut from ear to ear.'

'May the good Lord forgive me, but I cannot say I am sorry. He was a dreadful man.' Panic flashed across the footman's eyes. 'Though I did not kill him, if that is what you are thinking.'

'Calm yourself, Joseph, I have no suspicion in that quarter. Though I think you may know more than you are telling. I find it hard to believe you didn't know Steps was in Bridgnorth before you visited him on your mistress's behalf.'

'I did not.'

'Are you sure?'

'On my life.'

'And you didn't tell him where Mrs Beaumont kept her papers?'

For a moment, Joseph squared up to Edwin, his face red and his fists clenched, until the thief-taker raised an eyebrow. 'Really, Joseph, you are ready to take a beating? I've asked you once already to calm yourself and I now think you need to do so quickly. I have no quarrel with you, I simply want to know the truth. And I think you are still lying.'

Edwin stared hard at the footman, unspeaking. Joseph's breathing slowed and his shoulders slumped.

'I met him once. I had not seen Steps since I left home and entered into the Beaumont's service. As I told Meg, we had fallen out because of his dishonesty. About six months ago my mother became ill and I was out for the evening drowning my sorrows. My friends all went home and left me drinking alone. One minute I was by myself, the next Steps was sitting opposite me. I cursed him and told him to go but the ale took over and soon we were like old friends.'

'And this is when you betrayed your mistress?'

'I meant no harm. You must believe me. I was drunk and Steps wormed his way into my head. He asked where I worked, though I think he already knew. He asked many things.'

'Did he want to know where your mistress might keep her most precious possessions?'

Joseph screwed up his eyes and rubbed his cheek. 'Now I think of it, he did, in amongst so many other questions. Nothing seemed amiss at the time. I think I said they would be in her dressing room. How was I to know he would go looking for them? We parted company and I did not see him again. When I was sent on the errand by my mistress, I did not know who I was to meet, only the place he would be. She told me he would return a package, but he didn't. It was only when I saw his face I knew him, and straight away realised my mistress's troubles were not over. I only wish I had shown the courage to press him further. Perhaps then he would not be dead.'

'You think Mrs Beaumont had something to do with his death?'

'I dearly hope not, but how could it not be so?'

'Rest assured, Joseph, there are plenty besides her who would not be sad to see his demise. Other than the errand you described, is there anything else to point to her being guilty?'

Joseph shook his head. 'Nothing. It is good to hear you say there could be others. I have been worried it was her and she would be found out.' He looked over his shoulder, back to the house. 'May I go now?'

'I think we are about finished.'

The footman turned to open the gate, but Edwin touched his elbow.

'Before you leave. The girl, Meg, you like her?'

Joseph blushed and lowered his eyes. 'I do, sir. Very much.'

'Good, I am glad to hear it. But tell me this. Do you trust her?'

There was a pause, and Joseph frowned, as Edwin had seen him do before when he was thinking. After a few seconds, a grin spread across the footman's features. 'Yes, sir, I believe I do.'

Sarah had suggested meeting Edwin on the carters' track by the Severn. She walked it most days and knew they could so without raising suspicion. Her husband had business interests along the river, so what could be more natural than her delivering a message to one of them on her morning walk. He often asked her to do so if he did not want the bother himself.

She had no fear of bumping into Aubrey today, as he had ridden from the town at daybreak to carry out his duties in Shrewsbury, and he would be gone for two full nights. Nonetheless, she would need to be careful to avoid prying glances, especially those of Aubrey's cousin, Walter Downes, who occasionally spent time in the boatyards.

The track was alive with activity at this time of day. Workmen made their way between the different yards, and waggons loaded with coal and iron parts headed to the piers for transport up and down the river. One loaded with timber planks trundled in front of Sarah, and she only saw Edwin when it turned into a boatyard on her right. He bowed slightly and she could see he was better dressed than usual, despite the setting. A compliment she appreciated.

'Good morning, madam.'

Sarah glanced around and then leant forward, lowering her voice as had become their custom. 'Come Edwin, let us pause this pretence for a while, we are unlikely to be overheard amongst this hubbub. Being seen would be a different matter, but as long as we maintain a respectable difference we are just two acquaintances who have met by chance.'

'As you wish.'

Edwin took his place at her side, and they picked their way along the track, keeping clear of the mud-filled holes and dung piles.

'You wanted to see me, Edwin?'

'I *had* hoped you might also want to see me.'

'You mean to settle my debt?'

He stopped in his tracks. 'Nothing could be further from my mind. If I had wanted payment in such a way, I would have accepted your earlier offer before you had time to give a second thought. Indeed -'

The upturned corners of her lips caused him to pause. 'You are teasing me, are you not?'

Her smile turned into a full-blown giggle. 'You can be very self-righteous, Edwin. You do know this, I suppose?'

'I am pleased to give you such amusement, Mrs Beaumont.'

Rather than causing her to cease laughing, this only made her worse. 'Oh Edwin. Stop now. If we are to be ... friends ... you must not take offence at my silly jokes. They mean nothing other than affection.'

Edwin's features softened. 'I will try. Could I speak with you openly about a matter?'

'Of course, if you are easy with doing so, then nothing would give me greater pleasure.'

'Two days ago I asked you questions in respect of the murder of Ben Steps. This was contrary to my feelings for you, though it was completely necessary.'

'How so?'

'I am under considerable pressure from your husband to uncover the killer. I was reported to have been asking questions about him, on your behalf I might add, so stand accused myself if I can't uncover the real killer. Steps was attempting to extort money from me, as well as you and others, so a case could easily be made in court that I took his life.'

'And would that case have any validity?'

'None.'

'Then I understand the problem you faced. Think of it no more. Now may I ask you a question?'

Edwin nodded.

'You said you have "feelings." I believe you showed this when we were in my garden, but are they simply lust, like my husband's, or something deeper?'

'It cannot have escaped your attention, Sarah? My fondness goes far beyond what you suggest and has since I first laid eyes upon you. It is only the fact that you are married which has prevented me being more forward. Why do you think I was so angry when you offered yourself to me so cheaply?'

'At the time, I imagined it was simply because you wanted your money. Tell me this, the questions you asked of me, are you satisfied with the answers I gave?'

'I believe I told you I am.'

'Then we should put any unpleasantness behind us.'

A look Edwin could not quite fathom crossed Sarah's face before she continued. 'As for these "feelings" you mention, you must know they are reciprocated in no small degree. When we met in my garden, I did not take your hand in mine as a sister would.'

'Then what are we to do?'

'Perhaps if we walk together from time to time, as we are today, we shall find a way of pursuing them without raising Aubrey's suspicions.'

Edwin opened his mouth to reply, but snapped it shut again as horror appeared in her eyes. Just as quickly her smile returned, but now aimed at a man who limped towards them. Edwin did not recognise him.

The man was well-dressed, though not grandly so, and displayed a quizzical frown when he spoke. 'Sarah?'

'Ralf, how lovely to see you.' She turned to Edwin momentarily. 'May I introduce you to my brother, Ralf Norris. Ralf, this is Mr Edwin Hare, an acquaintance of Aubrey's who kindly offered to accompany me when we met along the track. Aubrey asked me to deliver some instructions to one of his boatyards, but I had not expected so many of these rough workers to be about today and I became nervous. One cannot be too careful, can one? Aubrey tells such awful tales of the villains abroad in the town these days.'

Norris looked Edwin up and down. 'Indeed there are, Sarah. All sorts of rogues and reprobates frequent the streets. Some of them even appear respectable at first glance. I trust, Mr Hare, you are not amongst their number?'

Edwin's features hardened, and Sarah stepped between the two men. 'What a rude thing to say, Ralf. Please apologise immediately.'

Her brother stepped back but continued to glare at Edwin. 'There will be no apology, Sarah. When I see my married sister walking with someone other than her husband, with a man I have never met, I believe I have the right to question his credentials.'

Edwin nodded. 'Your brother is correct, Mrs Beaumont, he clearly only has your safety at heart. I cannot quarrel with him for that. It is only natural.'

'Then the two of you must shake hands and be friends.'

Norris glanced at the hand offered by Edwin, then shook his head. 'I am sorry, sir, but I still know nothing about you. My sister is very dear to me, and you are accurate in your assessment that I would die rather than see any harm come to her. Now that we have been introduced, I will make enquiries, and if I hear your character to be good, then we may perhaps resume on better terms. Until then, I think it will be better if I walk with my sister from here and you make your own way to whatever you need to be doing today.'

Without waiting for a reply, Ralf Norris linked Sarah's arm and the two left Edwin staring after them. He wondered why the brother's name was on the list he'd retrieved from Ben Steps' home.

Nineteen

When Edwin turned into his lane, he saw a figure leaning against the wall of his house. It was Quentin Goode. The man coughed so much he could not get out any words until Edwin took him by the elbow and seated him inside.

Eventually, a slight colour returned to his grey face and his breathing eased. 'Thank you, sir, I do not know what I would have done if you had not come along when you did.'

'You are welcome, Mr Goode. Had you come to see me, or were you simply passing my door when the attack came upon you?'

'Indeed, it was you I wished to see. Your visit got me to thinking of my conversation with Ben Steps. Though we drank much, and I could remember little of it, odd pieces came back to me when I concentrated.'

'And you have remembered something which may be of use to me?'

'I hope so. Steps was unpleasant and a villain in many ways. But I believe I owe it to his father that I should help you catch the man who did killed him. Do you know a man by the name of Indigo Trussle?'

'I do. He works in the grain-store down by the river. A clerk I believe. From time to time he also helps in the magistrate's court, where I have spoken to him once or twice. Why do you ask?'

'Because Steps was boasting of how he made a living and said, by way of example, he was getting a pretty penny out of this man Trussle.'

'Do you know why?'

Goode shook his head. 'I do not. Either Steps did not say, or the gin has washed it away. As I said, we drank enough to kill a mule. Next day I thought my head would never again cease aching.'

'But you are certain now that Steps mentioned this man's name?'

Goode now grasped the arms of his chair and rose as if to leave. Before he could take a single pace, he clutched a hand to his chest and began to wheeze once more, falling back to his seat.

Edwin walked to a cabinet hanging in the corner and pulled a bottle from inside, then poured the brown liquid into a mug and passed it to Goode. 'Drink this. It is brandy and will calm your lungs.'

His visitor did as he was told and sat for a few moments breathing deeply. Goode rubbed his eyes. He drained the last drops and handed the mug back to Edwin. 'I must thank you once again, Mr Hare, though I was about to leave. It came close to an insult when you questioned my story. I am known by many as an honest man, not taken to lying.'

'My apologies, Mr Goode, if you gained such an impression, it was not my intention. You said yourself that your memory of that night is hazy, I merely wished to be sure you were not mistaken.'

'I was not, but I accept your apology. This damned distemperature makes me intolerant and I bark more quickly than I should.' He stood again and made for the door. 'Now, I feel much better thanks to your ministrations, and will take my leave. If I remember anything further, I may call on you again.'

As Goode stepped out into the lane, Edwin thought the memory would need to come soon, for, likely as not, the man would be in the ground before the month was out.

Edwin had called me to the side gate as I was finishing my lunch by the stables. He asked me to speak on his behalf to Walter Downes, my master's cousin, and told me the questions I must have answered. The thought filled me with dread.

'I don't think I am yet ready to take on such an important task, Edwin. Surely it would be better if you did it yourself,' the memory of being excluded from his conversation with Quentin Goode still annoyed me and I wasn't willing to let him forget his promise, 'and let me observe this time.'

He'd shaken his head. 'I haven't the time to speak to Downes and I have to make progress quickly. There are others on Steps' list to be questioned and I must spend half a day or more chasing after one of them.

This man's station in life requires I attend to him, otherwise I would send you in my place. If I did not think you capable, I would not entrust you with talking to Downes. What is it that bothers you?'

I'd explained there were two things, my uncertainty about what I should say, and the very real chance I could lose my job if Downes became angry and told my master.

'As for the first, Meg, I have said I trust you, and I do. If you are silver-tongued enough to convince me to train you, then I am certain you will have no difficulty with Mr Downes. I am so convinced this is true; I am willing to recompense you with a half a year's wages if the worst happens and you are dismissed. This will allow you either to seek other employment at your leisure or, should the fancy take you, become my assistant until you are ready to make your own way in the business of thief-taking. Now, will you do as I have asked?'

His offer had caused my objections to fly away like swallows at the end of summer, and I found myself speechless. Which is how I came to be following Walter Downes from my master's house and seeking an opportunity to attract his attention down at the boatyard. I knew Edwin to be now away to speak to Sir Thomas Weale, and he wouldn't be available to come to my aid if I needed him.

Downes, just like last time I'd followed him, exchanged words with men in the yard and gave them instructions to load goods onto a cart. When this was completed, and the men went back about their work,

Downes returned to the lane, and I stepped into his path.

'Sir, may I have a word?'

A tall man, he looked down at me over the rim of his spectacles and sniffed. 'Do I know you, girl?'

Should I tell the truth? 'I don't think so, sir.'

'Then what do you want with me?'

'I've been sent on an errand to ask a few questions.'

'Questions?' He looked me up and down. 'What right does a shabby thing like you have to ask me questions?'

My inclination was to kick him in the shin, though this wouldn't help in my search for information. 'I apologise, sir, I perhaps came at it a bit too quick. I'm only new to this trade and don't have the words like a man such as yourself. Please forgive me. I should've explained I'm sent by Mr Hare; I think you know him.'

'In a manner of speaking. We have met on a number of occasions, and I know which trade he is engaged in. What questions would he have of me?'

'It is a simple matter, Mr Downes. You may have heard that a man - Ben Steps - has recently been found dead. A list of names put together by him has come into the possession of Mr Hare, and yours is one of them. He has requested you tell me where you were on Monday in the early evening.'

'The man has a damned cheek, and I will speak to my cousin, the magistrate, about him. However, it is an easy one to answer. I was visiting my family in Much Wenlock. I left home in the morning, stayed to sup with my aunt, decided it was too late to ride back, so stayed with her until first light.'

'You're sure of the day?'

'I am. It was the anniversary of my mother's passing, so not one I would forget and the reason I journeyed over there. I try to go on that day each year.'

There seemed little point in asking my next question, but Edwin had suggested it, so I went ahead. 'If I may ask you one more thing, sir? Did you know this Ben Steps?'

Downes made as if to walk away, fists clenched by his side, but then turned back red-faced. 'That villain tried to ruin my life, and I am glad someone took a knife to him. I hope they made him suffer as much as pain as he caused to others.'

'I expect he tried to get money from you?'

'Not only tried. I would have resisted his squeeze, but my cousin said we could not face the scandal. For myself, my name means little, to Aubrey Beaumont it means much more. I borrowed the money from him to pay Steps a sizeable sum, and now I am forever in Aubrey's debt. It appears I merely swapped one master for another.'

As he spoke the word "master" a look entered his eye. He pointed a finger at me. 'Now I have you. You said I did not know you, but you were lying. I have seen you at my cousin's house. Working in his garden.' The accusing finger became a fist shaking in my face. 'If you were a man, I would knock you down for your impudence but, make no mistake, your master will hear of it. I will let him deal with you.'

It took Edwin over an hour and a half to ride the six miles to St Chad's at Stockton, then a further half hour for the remainder of his journey. As he approached the grand gate to the inner part of the estate, he realised what danger he was courting.

The Weale family owned half of Bridgnorth and a vast acreage to the north of it. Penning Hall, home of Sir Thomas Weale, baronet and current Member of Parliament, loomed out of the mist and there was no doubting it was a seat of power and influence. If Edwin put a foot wrong, he knew he would be in serious trouble. As with Aubrey Beaumont, this was not a person to cross if he wanted to keep his livelihood as a thief-taker, or his freedom.

Edwin was not inclined to use the tradesman's entrance, but on this occasion, he waited for a minute to consider it. He decided he would have little chance of speaking to Sir Thomas if he was not bold.

A man perhaps ten years older than Edwin opened the front door when Edwin knocked.

'Sir?'

'I would like a word with Sir Thomas. Please tell him it is Edwin Hare, on behalf of the magistrate.'

The servant's eyes widened. 'Could you give me a little more information, Mr Hare?'

'I am afraid not. It is a most confidential matter, and I am certain your master would be unhappy if the entire household knew all about it.'

With the curtest of nods, the man asked Edwin to

wait and closed the door. A few minutes later he returned and told Edwin to follow him. The entrance hall matched the grandness of the building's exterior, with portraits on display and a wide central staircase. A polite knock on a side door brought a brusque command to enter, and the servant ushered Edwin in.

The man standing in the centre of the room appeared younger than Edwin had expected. Squat, bewigged, and red-cheeked, he looked the very image of the country gentleman satirised in the broadsheets circulating round the taverns of Bridgnorth. He did not invite Edwin to sit. 'Magistrate Beaumont has sent you?'

'Not directly, Sir Thomas.'

'Pray what does that mean, sir? Either he has sent you or he has not. You told my man he had.'

'I did not, Sir Thomas, I said I was here on the magistrate's behalf, which is true. A man has been killed, and he has instructed me to find who did it.'

'Then I cannot see what this has to do with me.'

'It may give you an inkling if I mention his name. Ben Steps.'

No expression showed on Weale's face. No surprise, no puzzlement. Nothing.

'You know him, Sir Thomas?'

'I believe I have heard his name before, and even though I know many people, I do not go around murdering them. Please explain how you think I have a connection to this man's death.'

'Your name was on a list Steps had written. He was trying to extort money from others on that list, for secrets he knew about them, so, naturally, it is appropriate to consider them as suspects.'

'Then I think you can strike me from your enquiries, sir, for I was not one of that man's unfortunate victims.'

'He was not pressing you for cash?'

'Of course not. As you are doubtless aware, I am a person of some standing in this community. My family has been its benefactors for more than one hundred and fifty years. It is ridiculous for you to suggest I would do anything to jeopardise our reputation and give this man, Steps, a hold over me. I am sure you have heard of situations where such a creature makes false accusations against men like me then attempts to squeeze them for cash. He had not tried anything of this nature so far but perhaps it was his intent.' Weale pulled a pocket watch from his waistcoat and consulted it. 'I believe I have nothing further to say on this matter and our business is done, Mr Hare.'

Edwin nodded. 'As you wish, sir. I have no idea of Steps' intent, so it may be as you suggest, you were merely a possible victim in a scheme in his mind.'

Weale called for his manservant to escort Edwin from the house, then, as the door closed, the politician opened a table draw and withdrew a single sheet of grubby paper. He read the contents, smiling when he noted Ben Steps' name on the bottom. He tore the sheet into scraps and scattered them on the fire.

Early next morning, Edwin leant against the tree

where we'd agreed to meet, in the lane beside the gate. A spot out of earshot of the house, but easy enough for me to slip out to when he made his daily visits to my master. I'd reported in much detail my conversation with Walter Downes, including his threat to tell my master of my questions.

'So, Downes spoke as if both he and Aubrey Beaumont were affected by Steps' threats?'

If I'd expected him to be concerned with the possibility of my imminent dismissal, then I was mistaken. I shrugged. 'Seemed like it. Why else would he talk of the value of their name, and why would my master help him pay to meet Steps' demands?'

'And he didn't reveal the nature of the hold Steps had over him?'

'No. He threatened to punch me then stormed away. I hadn't chance to ask him anything else.'

'Interesting. Yet the magistrate's name was not on Steps' list.'

'Perhaps Steps thought he daren't chance his arm with him directly.'

'Then why would he think he could get away with it with Sir Thomas Weale, a much more powerful man?' He scratched his chin. 'Something to ponder on. It wouldn't surprise me if Weale was lying though. It comes naturally to politicians. Nevertheless, you say Downes was not in Bridgnorth at the time of Steps' death?'

'That's what he told me. Should we believe him?'

'You are right to question his truthfulness, though I cannot help thinking it would be a little too easy to disprove if the man is lying. He said he visited family, so they would have to be complicit and vouch for him. Also, it would take hardly any investigation to find if he had been seen in the town on the evening when Steps' throat was cut.'

Edwin has a keen eye for the logic of a situation. It probably wouldn't have occurred to me to consider the likelihood of Downes telling the truth, only if he wasn't. And those two things are not the same. The first perhaps requires some faith in the basic honesty of people, a somewhat surprising trait in someone like Edwin who deals in dishonesty every day. Would it be of benefit in the trade of thief-taking?

'You have done well in this first task, Meg. Now we need to move on.' He pulled Steps' list from his pocket. 'There are other names on here we need to consider, and we must not forget the man, Trussle, mentioned by Quentin Goode. I will go to find him when I leave here. I suspect you are not able to accompany me?'

'If only I could. But my dad, and my master, would notice if I'm not at my work and then there'd be the devil to pay. Who else is there for us to talk to?'

He squinted to make best use of the failing light and ran his finger down the page, biting his lip as he scanned the names. Part way down he gave the slightest shake of his head, then moved on. Edwin folded the list and placed it back in his pocket. 'I'm beginning to think this list may be a distraction. We have spoken to almost everyone and it has not taken us forward.'

'Almost everyone? Then one of those left might still be our murderer.'

His face hardened. '*We* do not have a murderer, Meg. The magistrate instructed me to investigate, and you have attached yourself to my coat. Please do not attempt to correct my methods. If I say the list is of no further use, it is of no further use.'

I stepped back and glared at Edwin. 'Don't dare speak to me as your servant, Edwin Hare,' I pointed over my shoulder, 'I have enough of that on the other side of the hedge. I may have asked you to teach me, but I still expect to be treated properly. If you don't want my assistance then all well and good, I'll go back to my duties as under-gardener and not bother you again. I'm sure someone else will be glad of my help.'

Inside I was shaking with anger and frustration, and hoped tears would not come. At least until I could escape through the gate and into the garden.

I turned and walked away but Edwin caught me by the shoulder. 'Please stay, Meg, I'm sorry if I spoke hastily. I meant what I said about you performing your task well. You are a good pupil, and I am sure you will make a fine thief-taker, when you are ready,' he smiled, 'and a little less keen to run away when you are insulted. The words I spoke are as nothing to what you will receive from those you might accuse.'

This, I knew, was a turning point. If I continued into my garden, I would regret it for the rest of my life, for Edwin and I would be finished and I knew no one who could take his place. But, if I showed he'd the upper hand, he'd keep it forever. This would need to be played carefully. I put on my sternest face. 'You think you can charm this away, Edwin? I'm not at all happy with you.'

'I can see this, and I am sorry. What else can I say to make it better?'

'You can start by promising not to treat me in that way again.'

'I promise I will do my best. I can offer no more.'

'Then that will have to do.'

'You said "start," is there something else?'

'There is another thing. I want you to ask my master or mistress to allow me more time to work with you. Only when my duties with them are done, of course.' I paused for a moment, unsure if I should say what was in my head. 'You might make the request to whichever you think likely to agree.'

The look of annoyance flitted across Edwin's face again, then disappeared. 'I can see you have thought about this long and hard. I can also sense you know more about me than you have let on. I have already asked once for some of your time, but will have another word with Mr Beaumont when the opportunity arises.'

We both glanced towards the garden as St Leonard's bells rang out the hour.

Edwin cocked a thumb at the gate. 'You had better go and do your jobs before you get into trouble. I will find Indigo Trussle. Let us hope this is not yet another blind alley.'

Twenty

Sarah was not surprised to see Edwin again so soon on her morning walk by the river, though did feel a little disquiet that he always seemed to know where she would be. There were far fewer people than when they had last met there, so she felt less threat of discovery.

She nodded and curtsied, though dispensed with the formality immediately. 'Good morning, Edwin. You are out bright and early.'

'I have people to see today but wanted us to walk together. I guessed you would be down here.'

'You seem to be very good at guessing my whereabouts.'

'It is what I do, as you know. If I can stay one step ahead of wrongdoers, then my job becomes easier.'

'Is that what I am? A "wrongdoer"?'

'No ... no ... of course not. I only meant -'

Sarah clapped a hand over her mouth to stifle her giggles. She still wore a smile when the fit had passed. 'Do not fret, Edwin, I am only teasing.' She looked in all directions and content she would not be observed, she touched Edwin on the forearm. 'I ask you again not take offence, Edwin. It did amuse me, yes, but only in a friendly way, it was nice to see you drop your guard for a moment.'

'You still find me stiff, then?'

'Sometimes.' Sarah saw Edwin's jaw set. 'A little. I believe you try to be a kind man, but, like now, you often seem on the edge of wanting to fight. If you think on my words for a second, you must know I meant nothing by them. You were exactly the same with my brother when you were introduced yesterday.'

'Me? Mr Norris was most aggressive towards me and, if you remember, would not shake my hand even when I agreed he was correct to wish to protect you.'

'Then the two of you are as bad as each other. However, I spoke to Ralf last evening. I have never been able to keep a secret from him and explained that you and I are friends, perhaps even a little more. Also, I told him you are an honourable person and have assisted me. I hope he has now revised his opinion.'

'Is it wise to have been so open with him? Will he not go to your husband?'

'Ralf is older than me and had left Ludlow before my father fell into difficulty. He worked in the wool trade around the country and had some aptitude. Though not a wealthy man, he became comfortably off and could have helped my father, rather than him falling into Aubrey's clutches. My poor brother has never forgiven himself.

'He dislikes and mistrusts Aubrey intensely, because of the way he forced me into marriage to ease my father's debt. The two barely exchange a word if Ralf can avoid it. Our secret is safe with him, do not worry.'

They continued to walk until they reached the bottom of Cartway, where more people were about. Sarah pointed up the hill. 'We must part here, Edwin. Let me go ahead for a minute or two so we will not be noticed together.' She took a look around. 'I have enjoyed this. I will send a message with your young friend when I may be free again.'

A few enquiries had revealed that Trussle still worked in William Piper's granary down by the river, though this week the County Sessions were taking place, and he would be clerking there. This meant Edwin had to take the long haul up the hill then walk through the town to the court chambers behind The Crown Inn. When Edwin entered, three clerks sat a large table in the entrance hall, each writing carefully into ledgers. They stopped simultaneously and looked up.

The one nearest the door spoke to Edwin. 'Is there something we can help you with, sir?'

Before Edwin could answer, a roar of voices rose in the courtroom beyond, and the clerk held up a hand to indicate a moment might be required to wait for the noise to subside. When it had, he spoke again. 'Some poor soul is getting a difficult time by the sound of it. Now, sir, you were saying?'

'I need to speak to Mr Indigo Trussle. I'm afraid I only know the gentleman by name, I do not think we have met, so my apologies if we have and it is one of you.'

The two clerks closest to Edwin turned and looked at third. He blushed and lay down his quill. 'I am Indigo Trussle, sir. How may I help?'

Even in his chair, Trussle was a tall, young man. Dressed in a coat which had clearly seen better days, he seemed an unlikely subject of Steps' attention.

Edwin wondered if he had been brought to this state because of it. 'Do you have a place where we might talk in private?'

Trussle looked at the oldest of his colleagues, who nodded to a door behind them, then returned to his work. When the clerk passed through the doorway he had to bend his head low, almost losing his cap in the process.

The room was not much bigger than a cupboard, the shelves on each side stacked with what appeared to be legal papers. The two men stood only an arms-length apart, with Edwin's back against the door. Trussle glanced nervously at the exit whilst Edwin explained why he wanted to speak to him.

Trussle was breathing deeply when he replied. 'I heard of Steps' death. It is the talk of the watering holes. Other than my name being on a list, surely you would not imagine I killed him?'

'Are you saying you did not?'

'Of course.'

'Even though he was extorting money from you?' Edwin pulled a hanging thread from Trussle's coat. 'Money I see you cannot spare.'

'That creature was disagreeable and vile, and I hated him with all my heart. You are right to observe I had not a fortune even before he squeezed me dry. But this was where Steps was devious and clever. If you were rich, he would demand a king's ransom, if poor, he bled you drop by drop. No-one was safe from him.'

'So, you had good reason to wish him dead.'

'Right again, I did. But I did not kill him.'

'What hold did he have over you?'

Trussle shook his head and laughed. 'You think I would tell you this? I do not know you from Adam, other than by reputation, and the reputation of others of your trade. What is to say you would not use this knowledge against me. I have already been in thrall to one man, I am not about to put myself in the same situation with another.'

Edwin took a step forward and Trussle backed against the wall, the bravado gone from his face.

'For now, Trussle, I will ignore the slur you have made on my character. Suffice it to say there are two flaws in your words. Firstly, I already have you down as a possible murderer, so there is little in your past which could overshadow that. Secondly, I have no interest in correcting any wrongs you may have committed, only in capturing a killer. I need to do this to clear my own name. Blackening yours will not aid me in that task. If you are not guilty, then you have nothing to fear from me.'

The clerk rubbed his chin in thought, sighing when he appeared to reach a conclusion. 'I had been taking money from my employer. Mr Piper is a good man, there are none better, but he is too trusting. My wife, Peggy, became ill and the doctor's charges were crippling me, so I began to shave shillings from payments when they were made, and I would fiddle the books to make them balance. This is simple enough if you know what you are doing. Despite his generous nature, Mr Piper does not pay well, but to save my wife from worrying I told her that he had given me an increase. When she recovered, and the doctor had been paid, she expected the extra money to continue. Cheating Mr Piper was not difficult, so what else could I do but carry on?'

'And Steps discovered that you had been stealing?'

'He did. I do not know how, but he threatened to expose me. Even if my employer did not put me before the magistrate, he would surely sack me. When it became known, I would also lose my work in this place, and we would be destitute.

'The man you see before you now is poor, but no pauper, and I have been trying to return Mr Piper's money little by little without Peggy seeing a difference. I would say to you that I am not a thief by nature, only by accident. I am also not a murderer; I do not have it in me.'

'This is indeed a sorry tale, Mr Trussle, and one I am inclined to believe. If you can give a satisfactory explanation of where you were when Steps was killed, I think we can put this behind us.'

Edwin never ceased to be amazed at the vast differences in wealth of the residents of his adopted town. Where he had grown up there had been the great landowner and the rest eked out what living they could from their small, rented patches. There were vast estates here too, like that of the Weales, for there were landed gentry everywhere. Bridgnorth had its fair share of wealthy citizens similar to the Beaumont's. Beneath these, the town, with its court and its river trade, attracted a goodly number of lawyers, merchants and other professionals. All of these were vastly outnumbered by people on the edge of penury, working for a pittance, or dependent on the parish. The old and infirm, the families with too many mouths to feed.

These differences could be seen in the range of houses, as would be expected. Close to the two churches, and where the town bled out into the countryside, were where the grander properties lay. Spreading like fingers from the high street, and on the east side of the river in low town, lived the traders ad skilled artisans. The lowest of the low filled the gaps, as their hovels spilled one on top of the other down the slopes. Some even occupied caves scooped out of the red sandstone centuries earlier.

The home the Trussles occupied was neither the worst nor the best of the poorer dwellings, and the tidiness in comparison to its neighbours hinted at a family doing its best to keep a standard in the face of the odds against it. The two small children outside scurried through the open door when they saw Edwin approach the house. They reappeared hiding behind the skirt of a woman holding a baby.

'Mrs Trussle?'

She eyed him with an expression between inquisitiveness and suspicion. 'Who wants to know?'

Edwin told her his name and his business.

'Well, if my Indigo said he was home when he said, then he must have been, mustn't he.'

'I am sorry, but that is not good enough. I cannot just take his word for it.'

'I don't wish to be impudent, sir, but you should. He may be a lot of things, but a liar he isn't.'

Edwin sighed. 'It would be so much easier if you could confirm what he has told me.'

The baby began to cry, though quietened quickly when the mother rocked it. 'I doubt I can be of much help, Mr Hare, with Indigo working so much, and with looking after these little ones being all I do, one day looks much like another.'

The woman did not seem to grasp that her husband's continued liberty, and her entire future, might depend on her answer. Edwin reminded her of this then pressed her again to try to remember.

'It is no good going on at me sir. If I don't know then I don't know, it's as simple as that. She ruffled the hair of the youngest child still peeking from behind her. 'You may as well be asking one of these two for all the good it will do you.'

The child began to bawl, perhaps disturbed by such unwarranted attention from his mother, or by the continued presence of the stranger at the door. Mrs

Trussle turned to return inside, but Edwin asked her to wait for a moment. 'This is very important, madam, so if you remember anything, anything at all, which will prove your husband was here with you that night, you must let me know.'

The woman looked blankly at Edwin.

'If you do not, Mr Trussle may be heading for the gallows.'

Without a word, she bent and hoisted the distressed boy up on to her hip and continued on her way. Edwin was left alone and wondering if she was as stupid as she seemed or merely playing a part to put him off the scent. He resolved to keep her husband as a suspect until it was clearer in his mind.

Twenty One

The day had been a busy one, and it had become dark by the time Edwin left Aubrey Beaumont. His regular meeting with the magistrate had been longer and more fractious than usual. Edwin had confessed he had made little progress and that most of those he had interviewed could vouch for where they were at the time of Steps' death. Those who had not provided solid proof still had a plausible story, even if it was difficult to confirm.

Beaumont had not been sympathetic and reminded Edwin his head would be in the noose if he did not come up with a name soon. Edwin responded with words perhaps harsher than may have been wise in the circumstances. The two parted company with little civility.

Edwin left by the front door, and closed it behind him, but made his way round the side of the house in the hope of seeing Meg. He had promised to keep her informed and this seemed as good a time as ever. He could not see her anywhere, and even when he quietly called her name by the back garden gate, she did not appear. This made his mood darker than when he had left the magistrate, and he stalked out of Cliffe House garden with his head down.

In the lane, a few yards from the gate, a thicket of shrubs formed a pleasing area of greenery in the daytime, but at this time of the evening they loomed ominous and dense. A man's voice from the darkness stopped Edwin short. 'Hare.'

Edwin peered toward the sound. He could make out nothing more than a pale oval where the man's face would be, and the merest glint of light reflecting from something at his throat. A chain? A necklace? Edwin took a step forward.

'Wait right there, thief-taker. I am armed and will not hesitate to shoot if you try to see me.'

The voice, undoubtedly a man, was deep and husky, though sounded disguised. Edwin stopped his progress. 'What do you want? I assume you mean me no harm or you would have shot without warning.'

'At present that is true. I will have no need to hurt you if you do as I ask.'

'What might that be?'

'Two simple requests. Not so much requests, as demands. Firstly, let sleeping dogs lie. There is nothing to be gained in your hunt for Ben Steps' killer.'

'And the second?'

'Stay away from Sarah Beaumont. She is a married woman and far above your station.'

Edwin laughed. 'You do not ask much, sir, do you? If you know anything at all of my business, you will be aware the magistrate has commanded I find the killer or face the consequences. Therefore, I can clearly not accede to your request in that respect. As for Mrs Beaumont, a lady I hold in high regard, I would beat you severely if you were to show your face. To suggest there is any kind of impropriety is insulting to both Mrs Beaumont and to me.'

'I did not suggest actual impropriety, but I am aware the two of you have been seen walking on more than one occasion and appeared closer than is seemly. Please heed my warning and stay away.'

Before he could reply, Edwin heard the rustle of leaves, and he guessed the man had made his way into the night. Unsure, he spoke into the darkness. 'Are you there, sir?'

Edwin received only silence as an answer. He walked cautiously to where the voice had been, but his knee collided with a fence within a few steps. So, the man must have been inside the boundary of the Beaumont's residence. Did this mean he was a member of the household and had watched Edwin leave? Joseph, the footman? Aubrey Beaumont himself? Or perhaps the cousin, Walter Downes, a regular visitor? He could think of no reason Joseph or Downes would want to warn him off a liaison with Sarah, other than loyalty to her husband. Maybe Downes had aspirations of winning her affections. As for the magistrate, he would have no need to accost Edwin under cover of night, even if he had time to get ahead of his target. In the heat of the argument earlier, a heartfelt "and keep away from my wife" would not have been surprising if he suspected anything. Also,

Beaumont could easily call off the search for Steps' murderer if he felt so inclined, with no need to threaten anyone. Instead, he had piled pressure on Edwin to continue.

Could the footman or Downes be more involved in the killing than Edwin suspected? He doubted it but would need to reconsider.

If the man who accosted him was not from the household and had simply followed him then lain in wait until he left, then it could be anyone. Anyone, at least, who had heard of him talking with Sarah and who had reason to try to stop his investigation.

Thaddeus Jackson had been one of the first to use Edwin's services. Edwin had known he would need to make contacts to establish his trade in a new town, and where better to do this than the inns and coffee houses? Jackson ran the White Horse tavern, was also a northerner, and loved the sound of his own voice.

One night, soon after they'd met, Jackson's usual good humour had seemed dulled, and Edwin had asked him what was wrong. He had opened out to Edwin that his purse had been stolen and, whilst no great sum was involved, it had annoyed him, and made him lose trust in his customers, something he could afford less than the money stolen. Jackson wanted to find the culprit to restore his faith in the majority.

Edwin had asked some questions and soon identified the man, a fool spending more freely than usual in another hostelry. Jackson settled for a profuse apology and the return of what was left, without involving the magistrate. Edwin had enjoyed free ale for a week or two, plus the innkeeper telling all and sundry what a great man Edwin was. A good deal of work had grown from this boost to his reputation.

Now, after Edwin's encounter with the man who had threatened him, he felt the need for a drink and good company, so found his way to the White Horse. There were few in the tavern, and those who were stayed huddled by the fire keeping their own counsel.

Thaddeus poured Edwin a mug of gin at his request. 'Stronger than your usual, Edwin. A bad day?'

'You could say so. Part of it is Ben Steps. Did you know him?'

'Was a customer, until I threw him out recently. Not the kind I want in here. Not surprised he met a bad end. What's he to you?'

'He is nothing, but his death is almost everything. If I do not find his killer soon then I will be hanged in his place.'

'Hardly seems fair.'

'Fairness has little to do with it. I was seen near his house not long before he was killed, and Steps had threatened me, so the magistrate has decided I could have been responsible. I am only holding him off from acting against me by searching for the man who did it, but all the tracks so far have come to a dead end.'

A tankard clattered to the floor at the far end of the room, its owner slumped, head down, at a table. Jackson shook his head. 'Another bad night for that one. Came in most evenings, bright and cheery. Chattering away to anyone who will listen. His wife died last month, leaving him with a newborn and three others to look after. Now he escapes in here once a week and drinks himself stupid. His eldest will turn up before long and take him home. I would refuse to serve him, but he would only go somewhere else. Somewhere his pocket might be picked. Or worse. At least I can keep an eye on him here.'

'You are a good man, Thaddeus.'

'I would hope so,' he laughed, 'I don't think I'm in the right business to be a bad one.'

'Perhaps you are right. You said you threw Steps out. Why?'

Jackson looked around the room and seemed satisfied his words would not be overheard. 'There is a man comes in from time to time, by the name of Frederic Allen.'

'The moneylender?'

'That's the one. I don't like him much, always something shifty about him, and he has a reputation of taking violent action to get his loans repaid. He drinks little but does plenty of business, especially in the days before the men are paid. He and Steps spent half an hour in discussion, one night about three weeks ago, then the chairs went over, and they were nose to nose with voices raised.'

'Do you know what it was about?'

'Everyone could hear. Steps owed Allen money and had not paid him. The moneylender pushed Steps and Steps pushed him back. I had to separate them. I sent

Steps on his way first, hoping they would calm down given a few minutes apart. As Steps reached the door, Allen shouted after him that he'd be sorry if he didn't come up with the money soon. Steps turned and shook a fist but then hurried outside, he must have known what was good for him.'

'Did Allen follow?'

'No, I sat him down, gave him a drink on the house, and, when he had finished, asked him not to come in again. He was not happy, but knows I have enough friends to make sure he would not cause me or my business any harm.'

Edwin asked if the tavern keeper had seen Allen in recent days, but he had not. Jackson topped up Edwin's mug and changed the subject. 'You said Ben Steps was only part of your bad day. What else?'

'Pfft. The usual.'

'A woman?'

'Of course.'

'Not something I hear you complain about, Edwin, you seem to have the pick of them.'

'This one is different. She is married and someone, not the husband, does not want me near her.'

'Then my advice is to move on. There are plenty more salmon in the Severn. Not worth getting your skull cracked over a pretty girl.'

Edwin threw back his gin in a single gulp. 'Perhaps you are right, Thaddeus. Now, I must go. I have things to think about.'

Twenty Two

Joseph's face was sour. He wouldn't often be told to work outdoors, and his expression made it clear he thought this beneath him. My master and mistress were expecting important visitors and wanted the front of the house to be perfect when they arrived in a day or two. We were two boys down, one having recently left and another with a cut on his hand which wasn't healing and had turned putrid. I doubted the lad would last the week.

As a result, my dad, working with a man borrowed from one of Mr Beaumont's tenants, was trimming the topiary and the parterre hedges. Joseph and I had been instructed to clear leaves, and to tidy the paths and lawns. Not heavy work but tiring, nonetheless. With every breath of wind, the job needed to be attacked again. The footman threw down his rake at the latest gust. 'This is a waste of time.'

'Welcome to my world, Joseph. I spend my days carrying out tasks which will only need doing again in the goodness of time, be it next week, next month or next year. That's how gardens are.' I pointed to my father and his helper. 'See, they cut back the bushes in the full knowledge the devils will grow again. The plants take no heed of our master's wish for order in his garden.'

Sometimes I wished I'd this in common with the plants I tended. A special kind of freedom, where even the lowliest of weeds could thrive despite the best efforts to keep them down or destroy them altogether. Where attempts at control were in vain.

Joseph's voice pulled me away from this musing. 'That's as maybe, and it might well suit you well enough, but my life is indoors. Clean and tidy,' he kicked a pile of leaves, 'and not made filthy again every time the elements take a tantrum.'

'But you're still a servant, Joseph. Just like me. Don't you want anything better?'

His eyes darted around the garden. 'Husht, girl, you cannot be saying such things.'

'Don't be so scared. The only ones who might hear us have their dreams too. So tell me yours.'

Joseph glanced round once again and lowered his voice. 'Of course I want to do better. I will not always be a footman. In a year or two I will move up in the household, even if I need to change my employer. Pretty soon I hope to become a butler. Then they will all bow and scrape to me.'

'And so, you'll still do a master's bidding, morning, noon and night?'

Without needing to say it, I knew that life wouldn't be for me. I equally knew it was the highest Joseph would hope for. A pity because I liked him, and I knew him to like me.

He replied with bitterness in his voice. 'I suppose you think you will be a grand lady one day, like Mrs Beaumont?'

'Not grand, Joseph, but better than this.'

I snapped more than I intended, and Joseph returned to his raking again, more vigorously than when he had left it. As I looked over at him, I spotted Edwin arriving for his morning report to my master. He nodded in my direction and looked tired, like a man with much on his mind.

I continued to clip the grass between the parterres but then I left my work, walked over to Joseph, and touched him on the arm, wearing the sweetest expression I could muster. 'I'm sorry. I didn't mean to sound cross. It's just I sometimes get annoyed with our lot. We're born into a poor life, and it often feels we can't climb out of it. To make something better of ourselves. It wasn't you I was angry with, only how you're accepting of your place in the world.'

His reluctant nod showed me we could still talk, and he might be persuaded to reveal anything he had heard indoors which had not been told to Edwin. I put the smile back in place. 'May I ask you a question, Joseph?'

He grinned from ear to ear. I'm not sure what question he expected me to ask but he nodded more energetically.

'Has Mr Beaumont said anything about this murder?'

His face fell. I'd only asked him for gossip. Joseph

shrugged. 'Why would he talk to me, other than to give his orders? I know only what everyone does. Ben Steps was cut from ear to ear, and Mr Hare is suspected of being involved somehow, though I do not believe it for a moment.'

It seemed better to pretend I held the popular belief. 'Why not? I heard he was seen sneaking from Steps' house.'

Joseph grinned. 'Nonsense. That is just rumour. Two facts tied together to make a pig's foot of a story. Though nothing has been said to me directly, I overheard a conversation between Mr Hare and the master. Even Mr Beaumont accepted the only evidence against him was he had been seen asking questions about Steps. Someone had been seen leaving the house but there was nothing to prove it was Mr Hare.'

'So, if not him, then who?'

'I think there are plenty wanted to see Steps in his grave.' Joseph cast a glance round the garden again before continuing. 'Even our mistress.'

'Mrs Beaumont?'

'I've worked that out from my own experience. She asked me to recover something from him. Something I guessed was especially important to her. When he would not return it, she begged me for his address.'

'Did you give it to her?'

'Eventually. I am not in the habit of disobeying her. I could not know the man would end up dead.'

'You can't believe she killed him.'

Joseph shook his head. 'Not really. I cannot see her

killing anyone, she is too gentle a soul. I only mention it to show even she had a reason and might create the opportunity if she wished. It could as easily be her brother. I attended the pair of them in the drawing room before Steps' death. Our mistress appeared to be wiping tears away when I entered, and they both stayed silent until I left. I listened at the door and heard her saying "what shall I do, oh, what shall I do?" Mr Norris replied she should not worry, and these things have a way of working themselves out.'

'And you think this meant he might harm Steps?'

'I would not go so far. I'm not sure they were talking of Steps and, again, I am only saying there are others besides Mr Hare who may have better incentive to murder.'

Before I could ask anything further, Dad whistled, and his scowl told me I should get on with my work. I leant in towards Joseph, as if to give a final whisper in his ear. Instead, I kissed him on the neck. When I pulled away his eyes were wide. 'Thank you, Joseph, you have been very helpful.' I winked. 'We will need to talk again soon.'

Only a few minutes had passed since he went inside, but Edwin came out of Cliffe House and crooked a finger to call me to him. 'The magistrate instructs that you help me today.'

I almost dropped my shears with excitement. 'You spoke to him?'

'I asked and he obliged. He is not happy but thinks he can do without the services of a mere girl for the occasional day if I have need of you.'

Whilst still an insult, I could see the advantage of my master thinking so little of me he could spare me to do what I actually wanted to do. 'Give me a few minutes to put away my tools and clean myself up. I'll be with you in a flash. You might have a word with my dad while I'm up there.'

Edwin opened his mouth as if to object, but I didn't wait. I rushed to my loft to brush myself down and change my hat. Without the luxury of a second set of clothes, I'd have to make the best of what I wore. As promised, I was back down the stairs in no time.

When I turned the corner, Edwin and Joseph were talking and a note passed between them. Edwin spotted me and quickly turned away. He walked in my direction and looked me up and down. It took all my effort to hide the grin I felt inside.

'Well, some improvement. At least there's not too much mud on your boots, but I would have preferred you looking a little more ladylike for this task. We will need to look into that for the future. Now, there are some matters which demand my attention, so I need you to talk to a man, Frederic Allen, who was seen arguing with Ben Steps over money. I believe him to be a nasty piece of work and I should really talk to him myself. You will need to avoid annoying him. Tell him I have sent you. That should give you some protection. Can you do this?'

I wasn't at all sure that I could, but I didn't want to tell Edwin so. 'Of course. I spoke to Walter Downes, and he was at least as scary.'

'Then go, and come to me this evening at Whelan's

coffee house, around seven o'clock, where we will sift through what we each have found.'

TWENTY THREE

Whilst he waited for Sarah on High Street, Edwin kept watch for anyone who might ask questions. It was as well he did. He had not been in position long when he saw Ralf Norris leave a coffee house across the street and make his way in Edwin's direction. Edwin ducked behind a market stall and Sarah's brother passed by, apparently without seeing him. Thankfully, Norris' path took him away from Cliffe House, or else he could have bumped into his sister and offered to walk back with her into town.

Edwin followed Norris briefly at a distance to ensure he continued his journey and did not turn back towards Cliffe House. Norris was easy to keep in view due to the mismatch in colour between his hat and cloak. The latter appeared superior quality and a deep red, different to the one he wore when they had met by the river. His hat, in contrast, was well worn and brown. An ill-chosen combination.

Edwin let him wander out of sight then returned to his planned meeting place. The church bells were ringing out ten o'clock when Sarah came to him.

Once she was sure they would not be overheard, she stopped the pretence of a casual conversation. 'I cannot stay long, Edwin. Aubrey is at home, and he will ask questions. You really should not have risked giving one of the servants a message. I hope it is important.'

'Something has been going round in my head, and I needed to ask you a question.'

'And it could not wait?'

'I have no time to waste. Your husband will have me before the bench within a day or two if I cannot find Steps' killer.'

'Then ask your question but be quick.'

'Could he have known about your lost letters?'

'Aubrey? We have been through this once already, Edwin. I cannot see how he would know and not reproach me. It would be the perfect excuse for him to get rid of me and keep Hannah.'

'But what if he wanted to protect your reputation. And his own. It would not reflect well on him if it became public knowledge the child may not be his.'

Sarah pressed her hands to her cheeks. 'Then I must get away, Edwin. You have to help me.'

'Why?'

'Do you not see? He would have me out on the street in a second if he could. If he has calculated it is more advantageous to avoid a scandal, then he will dispose of me some other way.'

'Are you saying he might kill you?'

'What else would he do? You already think he could have murdered that awful man. He would make it look like an accident, of course, or he would pay some footpad to attack me when I go out walking.'

'Before we jump to this conclusion, you must think, Sarah. Is there a way he could have known of Owen Ambrose's correspondence with you? If not, then you are safe. At least for the time being.'

'I did not think *anyone* knew about those letters, but some traitor did, and they told Ben Steps. Aubrey would not have stolen the letters and given them to Steps, it would serve no purpose.'

'Steps may simply have come across them by chance when searching for other valuables.'

'But this still means there is a viper in the nest. Someone told him where to look. When I find who it is, they will pay – with their job if it is a servant.'

Edwin steered away from exposing Joseph. The lad had revealed secrets without any malice. Drink will do that to a man. 'Did you ever discuss your past life with Aubrey? Could he have surmised the relationship with Owen Ambrose was more than a simple childhood friendship.'

'I never talked with my husband about Owen. He never asked about my past, nor I about his.' Sarah's voice shook. 'This is unbearable, Edwin, you are asking me to believe Aubrey knows of my relationship with Owen, and I have servants I cannot trust.'

'I am not asking you to believe anything, only telling you where the facts point. I beg you not to leave now. The servant will be easy to deal with if you uncover them. Your husband will be more difficult. If you run away, he will find you, regardless of what you might think. Then, as you have said, he will divorce you and take away your daughter. Allow me to continue my work, and we will see where it leads.'

A woman's voice called across the street. 'Mrs Beaumont, are you unwell?' The woman, twice Sarah's age, scurried over. She looked to Sarah, then Edwin, and back again. 'Why, my dear, you are quite flushed. Is this person bothering you?'

Sarah fluttered a hand. 'No, no. He is an acquaintance of my husband. We met in the street, and he was telling me of crimes he has recently heard of. One was a most grisly murder, and the story quite unsettled me. I am fine now and will be even better when you and I walk together to share more pleasant news.'

She linked an arm with the woman and nodded to Edwin. 'It was nice to talk to you, Mr Hare. I will tell my husband we met and will pass on your good wishes.'

Within seconds, Sarah was steering her companion down the street toward home.

Frederic Allen's house wasn't as large as my master's but certainly a cut above the rest. Part of a terrace which looked newly built, it had five large windows and an imposing front door. I found myself shaking when I knocked at it. The maid who answered surveyed me with barely disguised disgust. 'Yes?'

'Pardon me, miss, but I have been sent by my ...' what was Edwin? 'Er, by my employer. To have a word with Mr Allen. Is he at home?'

'He is at home, though I am not sure he will talk to the likes of you. Who is your employer?'

'Mr Edwin Hare, thief-taker. Tell your master Mr Hare couldn't come himself this morning but will do later if he won't speak to me.'

I tried to speak politely, but with a hint of threat to ensure I didn't have the door slammed in my face.

The maid raised her eyes to the heavens. 'Wait here, girl, and I will ask him.'

She disappeared and returned a few moments later, clearly unhappy with the instruction she'd received. 'Mr Allen has said you may come in. Wipe your feet and don't touch anything.'

She led me down a hall to a bright room at the back. A window overlooking the garden framed the man I assumed to be her master. He wore no wig, and his clothes suggested he spent more of his money on his house and furnishings than on his wardrobe. He waved me forward and then stared until it became uncomfortable. 'You can tell Hare he has a cheek sending a servant to talk to me. What does he want?'

The man was already in a bad mood, so I did my best to salvage his opinion. 'I'm sorry Mr Allen, sir, I did suggest to Mr Hare he should see you himself. But you clearly know him, sir, and when he takes a view he's not easily swayed. If you'd rather I left and ask him to come himself, I will.'

Allen bit the knuckle of his index finger and lost himself in thought for a moment. The chiming of a clock on the mantelshelf pulled him out of it. 'No matter. Tell me what he wants to know, and I will oblige if I can. There is little point in wasting time.'

'Thank you, sir. I'm sure this'll be cleared up easily. Mr Hare's been told, by a reliable source, that there was bad blood between you and Mr Ben Steps. Is that right?'

'Steps? The murdered man?'

'The one, sir.'

'Bad blood is perhaps too strong. He owed me money, could not pay, and I was, how shall I put it? Disappointed.'

Allen affected the manners and speech of a gentleman, but I understood him to have humbler beginnings, only gaining a fortune through his endeavours as a moneylender.

'Mr Hare heard there'd been an argument, with violence and threats.'

'He caught me in a poor mood. The amount he owed was not significant, but I wanted him to know he had to pay.'

'Or else?'

He clapped his hands. A single clap, but emphatic. 'Hare thinks I killed him. How interesting. But what would be the point? With Steps dead I would not be paid, would I?'

Bravado got the better of me. 'To teach him a lesson, sir?'

His laugh sounded cruel. 'It is clear you know little of the world, young lady. If I wished to teach Steps a lesson, I would have had him beaten by some of my boys. That way, he would learn, and he could still pay his debt. Others would also be reminded not to try to take advantage of my good nature. I am surprised Hare would think otherwise. He must believe I have become softer as I have grown older.' Allen turned his back on me and looked through the window. 'You had best tell him this is not the case.'

There was certainly logic in what he said. But, then again, murder is perhaps not such a logical action. If Allen would have a man attacked, as part of a business arrangement, who knows what he might be capable of if he lost his temper. On balance, I was tempted to believe him, but I'd make my report to Edwin and let him decide.

Without speaking to me again, Allen pulled a bell-rope to summon the maid, who grinned all the way as she led me to the street.

Down by the wharf it was as busy as when Edwin had last walked there with Sarah. Carts, horses, men, women, and children everywhere, a myriad of activity. He found his way to the riverside after Sarah went off down High Street with her new companion. Unsure where to go, other than avoiding the four walls of home, he carried a vague hope the walk would help clarify his thinking and unpick the knot of threads which made up this mystery. It seemed like none of the strands led anywhere.

His thoughts wandered as he made his way through the workmen and traders, and it occurred to him that everyone has a guilty secret, some more serious than others. The important question, as far as he was concerned, was who had something hidden which might destroy them financially or in terms of their reputation if it was revealed. Of the people on Ben Steps' list, who had enough to lose to make murder a better option than paying the man?

A boy with a sack-cart loaded with more than he could handle narrowly missed Edwin and swerved into a rut, splashing mud on the thief-taker's breeches. Edwin cursed. He bent to wipe the dirt off and spotted Walter Downes in the boatyard on the left. Instinctively, Edwin crouched lower so as not to be seen. Behind Downes, two men were unloading bales from a trow onto a waggon and he appeared to be keeping watch, surveying the lane in both directions. When he looked away to give directions to the workers, Edwin quickly moved to the side of a shed where he could see but not be seen.

The men continued to pile up the waggon until Downes shouted for them to stop, then they covered the bales with sacking before leading the horse and its load out onto the lane, and away out of sight. Downes walked to the riverbank and appeared to pass some coins to the boatman before leaving, with a final glance around.

Edwin stepped out to stop his progress. 'That was an interesting scene, sir.' Downes attempted to walk round, but Edwin stood in front of him again. 'I assume your cousin knows you are removing his goods?'

'Of course. Not that it any of your business.'

'I imagine Mr Beaumont would say that it is very much my business. Not only do I work for him, but the work I do entails seeking out thieves and villains. In that case, I am sure he would expect me to look out for his best interests.'

'Then worry yourself no more on that account, your employer is well aware of what I am doing. Now, I have no desire to answer your questions any further, so I will be on my way.'

Downes side-stepped again but Edwin grabbed his arm, easily resisting the attempt to shake him off. 'You will speak with me, sir, or I shall drag you up the hill to Mr Beaumont where you will account for your actions. It looked for all the world as if you had something to hide. Were you stealing from the yard?'

A look of disgust appeared on Downes' face.

'Stealing? Me? Why should *I* be stealing? You have shown how easy it is for such a thing to be witnessed in broad daylight. If I had any intentions in that way I would do it less in public view. Take me to my cousin if you wish, he will only confirm I had his permission.'

'Then why the subterfuge? You were quite obviously trying to ensure you were not seen by someone.'

Downes finally managed to wrench his arm from Edwin's grip, pulled himself to his full height, which was till several inches shorter than his questioner, and tugged at the front of his topcoat to straighten it. 'The person I was attempting to avoid was the customer for whom the goods were intended. If you wish to know more, I suggest you speak to Aubrey.'

'A customer? Why would -' the thought hit Edwin like a lightning bolt. 'Ah, the good magistrate is stealing the bales himself, getting you to do the dirty work.'

Downes did not reply.

'I surmise he takes the materials, sells them on to another customer, and tells the first his must have been stolen in transit or were never delivered. Extra profit, reduced only by a shilling to the boatman and I expect a small payment to you.'

'I did not tell you this. You must not say to Aubrey that I did.'

'Do not be concerned, Mr Downes. If the cheated customer does not come for my services, then I have no interest in bringing the thief to justice. Which, in this case, may be a little difficult as the magistrate is both culprit and law-bringer. However, I am sure you wish to avoid any unpleasantness from me involving your cousin. I can pack this information away until I need it, which may be soon enough.'

Downes tipped his head in acknowledgement.

'So, all you have to do, Mr Downes, is give me something else I may use if I need a bargaining chip.'

'Like what? You would know him as well as anyone.'

'Yes, but you have known him longer. I believe he only appeared in Bridgnorth in his early twenties. Where was he before that? Where did he come from?'

'I can tell you he and I grew up in Whitchurch, in the north of the county, but I will tell you no more.'

Whitchurch. The same town where Quentin Goode

was born.

Twenty Four

Quentin Goode appeared in no better health than the last time Edwin spoke to him. His cough was, if anything, even more violent, and his skin had become grey. When Edwin had knocked at Goode's door, he had simply croaked for him to enter, not bothering to rise.

Edwin enquired if Goode had enjoyed any improvement, but he just shook his head. This alone prompted another bout. The coughing fit over, Edwin explained the reason he had called. 'Do you remember a man named Aubrey Beaumont from your time in Whitchurch?'

Goode rubbed his whiskers. 'The magistrate? I cannot recall the name from there. Beaumont would not have been a local one.'

'He has a cousin, Walter Downes, perhaps he would be more familiar?'

'That is a name I do know. He now lives in the town I believe.'

'Indeed he does.'

'Then I think the other you mentioned is not

named Beaumont. Downes' mother only had one brother, and their family name was Roden, poor by any standard. The brother had two sons and a daughter. One son *was* called Aubrey, the other died of a fever at about sixteen years.'

'So, Aubrey Beaumont must be Aubrey Roden. But Beaumont is a wealthy man.'

'Even as a very young boy, he would always have something to sell if you met him. In the beginning it would be fruit or vegetables which he claimed to have found. Later it could be anything from a chicken to a horse - or tools. Despite this, the family never seemed any better off. One day, Roden was challenged that he had stolen a ploughshare which he was trying to sell, but he was able to bring forth the man who had sold it to him. It turned out he had been saving his money to buy things of greater value. That would be about the time I left Whitchurch to enter Sir Edward's employ. I expect that the lad would have been twelve or thirteen years old by then.

'Later, I heard he'd traded his way up to purchasing land and charging rents. By all accounts he was a hard landlord and would reclaim the land if the tenant fell into any arrears, then put someone else in at a higher rent. I expect Roden stole, cheated, and lied his way to a fortune.'

'Do you know why he left?'

'Seemingly, he chose the wrong family to intimidate, and three brothers came after him. They beat him 'til he could take no more. When they had finished, they told him he should move on. I heard no more of him being in Whitchurch after that day, though I did hear he had done the same in neighbouring villages. With his lack of scruples, he could have built a good pile over a short time. So this is our good magistrate? It is many years since I saw Roden, I would not have guessed he was Mr Beaumont.'

'He must have moved here with a new name, considerable wealth, and a ready built respectability. Though, from what I have been told, he has lost none of his greed. Did you ever hear of him using violence?'

'Not to my knowledge.'

Edwin paused to think of the implications. The man he knew as Beaumont would have had much to lose if he had been exposed by Ben Steps, yet he was not known for being violent. Had he changed in the intervening years? Edwin knew him to be calculating but he could also be charming and was a pillar of Bridgnorth society. Was such a man capable of murder?

When Edwin turned to ask Goode another question he saw the man had fallen asleep, so covered him with a blanket and left, lowering the latch as gently as he could.

The front door of Cliffe House opened. Ralf Norris stepped back on seeing Edwin standing outside. 'Why, Mr Hare, you startled me.'

'I apologise, sir, I was about to knock. I need to see your brother-in-law.'

Norris looked over his shoulder before speaking again.

'If it will wait a few moments, I would like to speak to you.' He gestured to the garden path. 'We should be private enough over there.'

Edwin let him pass, then followed. 'What is it you want, Mr Norris?'

'I wanted to say I am sorry for our last meeting. It seems I had misjudged you when I saw you walking by the river with my sister. At the time this seemed to me inappropriate, and I reacted accordingly. All I can say in my defence is that Mrs Beaumont is everything to me and I would do everything in my power to protect her. However, she and I have now spoken, and I am assured you have performed a great service to her. I am therefore also in your debt and hope you will forgive me.'

Norris smiled and held out his hand. Edwin took it but did not bother to smile. He welcomed the apology, and knew he could not expect any kind of future with Sarah if he was an enemy of her brother. Not yet ready to forgive Norris' snub, he gave the expected response. 'Think no more of it, sir, these things happen. You are to be commended for defending your sister's interests.'

The two men exchanged pleasantries for a short while, until Edwin made his excuses and returned to the door. Joseph answered and led him through to Aubrey Beaumont's room, where he was seated by the fire. 'Good God, Hare, what time do you call this? You are late reporting today.'

'I would call it the time for you to tell me what you know of Ben Steps.'

Beaumont stood. 'Are you a fool, man? I know only what I have told you already.'

Earlier, Edwin had ripped his own name and Sarah's from Steps' list. He now drew the remainder of the sheet from his pocket and thrust it in front of the magistrate's face. 'You see the fifth name down, Mr Beaumont?' He jabbed a finger at the spot. 'Here. The name Roden. Your true name, is it not?'

Edwin had never seen Beaumont so taken aback before. It was as if he had been slapped.

The magistrate sat down again, mopping his forehead with a handkerchief. 'How ... how did you find out?'

'I keep my ears open, and I make connections. That is why I am good at my job. Was Steps trying to extort money from you to keep this quiet? Or had he discovered about your little sideline by the river. I have to say I find it ironic that the man responsible for upholding the law is breaking it on a daily basis.'

Beaumont laughed harshly. 'You are so naïve, Hare. How do you think wealthy men stay wealthy? I am doing no more than we have done since time began. I see an opportunity to make money, and I seize it. The law is made to protect the rich, not punish us. Steps could not have embarrassed me by revealing my "sideline" as you put it. True, I may have lost a few customers, but they would not have taken the chance of prosecuting a magistrate. The judges and all the town burgesses are friends of mine or owe me money.

Who would my accusers find to try me?'

'I wish I had your confidence of being so much above the law. The day may come soon enough when that pride is tested. Are you saying Steps did not threaten you?'

'That is not what I said. The man came to me saying he had information about my activities, and I told him what I have just told you. Though not so politely. I sent him on his way and warned him never to come near me again or he would find himself deep in a dungeon until his hair turned grey.'

'And the change of name?'

'I do not believe he knew of this, and, even if he did, it is a small matter. I would have dismissed his threats with this as I did with the other.'

'You know, well enough, Mr Beaumont, it is not a small matter. People here believe you are who you say you are, a man of good upbringing, a man of the best stock. Not some pauper from Whitchurch with intellect, wile, and poor morals.'

Beaumont slumped in his chair and wiped his brow again. His mouth moved like a fish out of water. No words emerged.

'Do not look so surprised, once he knew your name, my informant was able to tell me all about your past life. If this became known, you would not last long on the bench nor in society. Protection of a good name is something a man might kill for.'

The magistrate did not speak for a moment. When he did, steel had appeared in his eyes. 'So now we have it, Hare. You wish to point the finger at me to take the heat off yourself. Be careful. I still provide you with much of your work, and the rest comes because I tell others you are effective. If this was to stop, where would you be? Other thief-takers exist and would be more than willing to step into your boots. You also forget what I said earlier. I am a person of power and influence. No-one is going to take your word over mine. I did not kill Ben Steps; I had no reason to. But if I had, you would not convince any judge hereabouts to convict me.'

'You want me to believe you had nothing to do with Steps' death?'

'It is of no interest to me if you believe it or not. What *you* must believe is that I will act against you in the coming days. Find Steps' killer or face the consequences.'

Twenty Five

Edwin sat across from me at a table in Whelan's coffee house. Around us the other tables were occupied by groups of men, well-dressed and mainly bewigged. Most puffed away on clay pipes, a penny cup of coffee in front of them, whilst chatting with their companions. Snatches I overheard were of topics such as the weather, the state of the country's finances and the health of the king.

We had met in the evening, as agreed, to discuss what progress had been made during the day, but the anger Edwin wore when he arrived still hadn't gone. I'd asked him what was wrong, but he waved it away and turned instead to the question in hand. 'Who do we have then, Meg?'

After he spoke, he glanced towards my feet and when I looked down, a rat had pushed its snout from under a nearby wainscoting panel, sniffing the air. I threw my hand to my mouth, stifling a shriek and the vermin scurried across the floor. Edwin lashed out with his foot, but it swerved and squeezed itself under the door, to the amusement of the men on neighbouring tables.

I tried to lighten the mood. 'Do you mean other than you, Edwin?'

At least it raised a smile from him, even though he answered with sadness in his voice. 'This is the problem, Meg. I did not kill Ben Steps, but the Lord knows I had as much motive as everyone else on his list. And all we have is motive. No-one was seen, or, rather, someone *was* seen but not recognised. There are few who can prove where they were on the night Steps died, and all seek to be taken at their word.'

'Shall we look at those we've spoken to, and see if we've missed anything?'

'Do you not think I have not done that, Meg? Twenty times or more.'

'Then do it once again for my sake if nothing else. I still need to learn much from you.'

Edwin sighed and held up his palms at arms' length. 'If it will make you happy.' He smoothed creases from the list he took from his pocket. 'There are six names we need to consider. Indigo Trussle, Walter Downes, Frederic Allen, Sir Thomas, Sarah's brother - Ralf Norris, and this man, Roden. I will tell you about him later.'

'But I thought there were eight names on there, not six? Two are missing.'

'There were eight. The others are me and your mistress, so I removed them.'

'You've ruled out Mrs Beaumont?'

'I have. We spoke and I believed her.'

For the life of me I couldn't see why she should be

believed while others were assumed to be lying. Perhaps it was a dose of love-blindness, but I daren't argue. Edwin remained in poor temper and wouldn't take kindly to being contradicted on this topic.

His finger ran down the remaining names. 'I also tend to believe Allen and Trussle. The first told you he would lose more by killing Steps than having him beaten. If Steps had suffered a single stab wound, it could have been Allen's thug's threatening gesture gone wrong, but it was not, he was slashed from ear to ear.

'Trussle gave his wife to account for him. She appeared stupid and confused, but I can't see he'd say she would vouch for him if she couldn't.'

I asked about the Member of Parliament, Sir Thomas Weale.

Edwin frowned even more deeply than he had so far. 'I did not like the man, Meg. Not one bit, and I suspected he was lying. His name is clearly on here, but he denied Steps had contacted him. I need to find more about him. What did you think of Walter Downes?'

'He acted very suspiciously. It looked to me like he's stealing from my master. If he is, and Steps found out, Downes might try to silence him.'

'The difficulty with that argument is he is not stealing from Beaumont. Quite the reverse. He is robbing customers on the magistrate's behalf.'

'What?'

Edwin told me what he had learned from Quentin Goode about my master's false identity and his dishonesty. I sat open-mouthed when he revealed all of this. In the main I was disgusted that a rich man would want to be richer. A small part of me was dizzy with confirmation that someone who had beginnings as humble as mine could rise so high in the world.

Edwin shook as he talked about his recent discussion with my master. 'He threatened me, Meg, and I allow no man to get away with that. He will get his reward soon enough.'

I asked if my mistress knew of her husband's past.

'I find it hard to believe she would. How could she stay with him if she does?'

I wanted to explain to him he'd no idea of the lives of women. Mrs Beaumont stays because she has no choice. Her father is not a rich man and so she's no fortune of her own. Even if she did, it would be under her husband's control. If she were to leave him, she would have no means of support and precious few skills she could use to find work. The best she might hope for would be the charity of her family to save her from a life of servitude.

Though my blood boiled at Edwin's ignorance, I decided to leave him to it on this occasion. 'Do you think Mr Beaumont could have killed Ben Steps, Edwin?'

'He is adamant he did not, but so are they all. Again, we should not discount him just yet.'

'So, is Mr Downes still under suspicion?'

'Let us say he is further down the list than some others. He is a lapdog doing Mr Beaumont's bidding. Perhaps Steps only wrote him down as a possible target in the future.'

'Then this leaves us three. My master and Sir Thomas, the last being Mr Norris. You have not spoken of my mistress's brother.'

'Because I know little of him. We were introduced recently when he was aggressive towards me.'

'Aggressive how?'

'I met your mistress out walking, quite by chance.' It took a major effort to stop myself from raising an eyebrow, but I managed it, and he continued. 'We bumped into her brother, and he questioned me as to my motives. The man almost openly accused me of being a rogue. It was all done with a fitting level of politeness though there was no doubting his intent. Earlier this evening we met again. He was leaving Cliffe House and called me aside to apologise, but it did not feel entirely sincere. Apart from being on Steps' list, like so many others, I have no other reason to believe why he may wish Steps harm.'

Was this yet another example of a blind spot in Edwin's thinking, caused by his affection for Mrs Beaumont? 'You haven't spoken to him yet about it?'

'I have not had chance, but I will make a point of it soon. It was only when Mrs Beaumont introduced us that I recognised his name from the list.

'What about someone who isn't on Steps list?'

'This is a possibility, and you are wise to keep an open mind, Meg, but I think we have enough of a puzzle already, without complicating it further.

Edwin stood. 'Let's sleep on it tonight, Meg, perhaps it will be clearer by tomorrow. We have made satisfactory progress, so I will report to Beaumont in the morning, and we will talk afterwards.'

Edwin rose late. The night had been humid and thundery, so even if he had been able to shake the problems from his head, it would have been a sleepless one. A massive clap just before dawn was the last, and he managed to doze afterwards.

No solutions had come to him, his usual clarity clouded by thoughts of how he would repay Aubrey Beaumont for the threat he had made. The lack of bread in his cupboard reminded him he was running low on funds. Not yet desperate, but the money he had given Meg, and Sarah's still-unpaid bill, had not aided his finances. All of his time was being taken up by Steps' murder, and Edwin knew there would be no funds forthcoming if he caught the killer. The only reward would be saving his own neck.

His mood was low when he rapped on the magistrate's door, half an hour later than his usual time. Joseph led him through. Beaumont did not offer him a seat. This meeting would be formal, with Edwin sensing the magistrate eyeing him as if he was already in the dock. 'I believe I made a little progress last night, Mr Beaumont. We have whittled the field down to three.'

Beaumont raised an eyebrow. 'I trust I am not one of them?'

Edwin did not reply.

'It is of no importance; I am bored of this and your

incompetence. I will give you until noon tomorrow to put your affairs in order and I will then have you taken to the cells. Now leave me.'

'But you are not being reasonable, sir. You know, as well as I, that I did not murder Steps -'

The harshness in Beaumont's voice echoed the cruel smile playing on his lips. 'I have told you once I am not interested. I need to put someone's head in a noose, so it might as well be yours as anyone's. If you do not have the culprit by the allotted time you will hang. That's an end to it and I will be a happier man.'

Edwin shook his head. 'I fail to understand why my hanging would give you pleasure.'

'Do not look so shocked, Hare. Do you think I do not know about you and my wife?

'There is nothing to know, sir, and you impugn your lady wife seriously by suggesting such a thing.'

'At present, perhaps. My sources say it is nothing more than flirtation so far, but I know it will become more if I leave you free. Putting you on the gallows will make the local citizens sleep more soundly and will rid me of any doubt about my wife's fidelity.'

'And it removes any suggestion that you are guilty of Steps' murder. How convenient.'

Beaumont turned to his desk and rang a small bell to summon Joseph. When the footman arrived, his master waved the back of his hand towards the door. 'Let Mr Hare out, Joseph. And do not let him in again without my permission.'

He returned to his desk and began to address some papers.

In the hall, Edwin stopped Joseph. 'I must speak to your mistress before I leave.'

The footman glanced at the door they had just passed through and shook his head. 'I dare not sir. The master will have me whipped.'

'I would not ask but I believe your mistress may now be in danger. Consider where your loyalty lies. Let me out into the garden, and I will wait a few minutes. If she does not come, I will know you have failed to speak to her. If she does, I will be forever in your debt.'

Joseph hesitated, then waved Edwin down a passage to a door at the rear of the house. 'Go through there, sir. Follow the path to the bench surrounded by shrubbery. That is Mrs Beaumont's quiet spot, and you will not be overlooked.'

Twenty Six

Sarah's face was flushed when she arrived. Edwin could not tell if it was due to the exertion of hurrying down to meet him, or if there was something else. Her first words showed it as the latter. 'You have done it again, Edwin. You have put me in jeopardy.'

'You were already in jeopardy, madam. Your husband knows that we have been meeting.'

'You told him?'

'Not I, but someone has. He just revealed it to me.'

She leapt up and glanced towards the house. 'Then he must not see me with you now.'

'We will not be observed, Sarah, please sit. Joseph is keeping watch and will warn us if Aubrey leaves his room. You need to reward your footman for the risks he's taken on your behalf.'

'I think that is perhaps the least of my worries. Aubrey will have me out on the street if he hears of us together again. I must act now and end this. You must go, Edwin.'

'Wait another day. That is all I ask. If I can find who murdered Ben Steps by tomorrow, then you and I will leave together.'

'Oh, Edwin, you understand nothing. I cannot leave Aubrey. Not only would he dispossess my father, who still owes him money, but you and I would be penniless. We would need to move away from Bridgnorth, and I would lose Hannah.' Sarah rose. 'No, it is better that I go to him and ask for his forgiveness, tell him it has meant nothing, only the silly games of a silly woman.'

She ran from Edwin to the house. When she looked back, Edwin saw the tears on her cheeks.

From the corner of the garden, I saw my mistress go inside through the back entrance. She appeared to be crying though I was too far away to see properly. Mrs Beaumont had looked towards the place where she usually sits when the weather is fine. I caught a glimpse of movement so watched for a moment. Edwin came out. It shocked me that he'd been so bold as to speak with my mistress in full view of the house. When I called out to him, he looked almost as surprised to see me.

He hurried over to where I'd been working. 'Did you hear any of our conversation, Meg?'

Not a "good morning" or any semblance of other greeting, just concern if he'd been overheard. I wondered if he saw me as an assistant at all, or simply a dogsbody to do the jobs he hasn't time for.

'I heard nothing, Edwin. I didn't even see you until you came out. I won't ask why you were in the garden with my mistress.'

'How dare you presume ...,' he drew breath when he saw the anger in my eyes, 'I am sorry, I should not have spoken in that way. I am out of sorts this morning.'

Though he'd said the words, there was no real apology in them.

'I needed to tell your mistress something important.'

'So, you haven't changed your mind and decided to question her more about Ben Steps?'

'No.'

'Why not, Edwin? If she was on his list and can't prove where she was when he died, she should be as much a suspect as anyone else on it.'

'I have told you already, I am satisfied she is innocent.'

Once again, I was expected to take him at his word. 'That's as maybe, though perhaps you should explain how you get to that decision. Otherwise, I might think it's because you've something going on with her.' I gave no pause for him to reply. He'd caused my blood to boil, and it hadn't yet reduced even to a simmer. 'I also don't understand why we're looking no further than that scrap of paper you found in Steps' house. All the people on there had a motive for wanting their torturer out of the way, even you, but there may be others. The list might be incomplete, or someone has a different reason to want Steps dead.

'I think you're being sloppy, Edwin, or misled, or beguiled by my mistress's pretty face. Why isn't she a suspect? Who could have a motive beyond those people we've spoken to? Why should I even believe you didn't do it? Convince me. We have a murder to solve.'

The thunder I'd heard in the night was nothing compared to that now on Edwin's face. 'Be quiet, girl. You know nothing. I have told you once, *we* do not have a murder to solve, *I* do. You are simply helping, and at the minute, not helping all that much with your stupid questions.'

'Stupid am I?' Then you don't need to put up with me any longer. I wouldn't want to get in the way of you taking the glory for finding who killed Steps.'

I turned and marched away and didn't stop when I heard Edwin's final words.

'Please don't go, Meg. You don't understand.'

'Can you figure out women, Thaddeus?'

'What man does, eh?' Beyond me is all I can say.'

Edwin had watched Meg leave the garden and join her father in the stables. He knew he could not follow her there. Instead, he dropped his head and found his way to the White Horse tavern, where Thaddeus Jackson had been reluctant to serve him gin so early in the day. Edwin insisted, threatening to find someone who would, so Jackson gave in. He sat with his customer to sweep up the pieces when they inevitably fell. Three glasses in, Edwin had become mellowed but not quite drunk.

They had talked of Ben Steps' killing before Edwin

had turned to why he was drinking. 'Y'know, Thaddeus, today I lost two of them. Told them both the truth but would they listen? No. Next thing, they are walking away saying they never want to see me again.'

The landlord laughed. 'Two, Edwin? What are you doing with two on the go at the same time anyway?'

Edwin frowned, then shook his head. 'Not like that, man. No romance with one of them,' he shook his head even more, 'no romance with either if truth be told. Not any longer. One was almost a friend, the other ... well who knows. It might have been.' Edwin stared at his empty glass. 'Give me another.'

'No more now, Edwin. From what you said earlier you have work to do.' He poured Edwin a jug of small beer. 'Here, drink this, it will help with the thirst.'

Edwin did as he was told and complied when Jackson led him outside by the elbow.

It was not many steps to his home, where the door creaked in on a room which was damp and cool. It felt lonely. Edwin threw off his hat and sat in a chair by the dead fireplace. He wanted to sleep but could not, the arguments with Sarah, Meg and the magistrate swirling round and round.

He drifted off. He was in a courtroom, with Ben Steps, shrivelled and rotting, pointing at him from the witness stand. Sarah and her brother stood as the prosecuting lawyers alongside Aubrey Beaumont. Neither Sarah nor Ralf were dressed for the court. She wore the finest of gowns and he his outside clothes, including hat and cloak. The pair laughed and repeating "guilty" over and over like a children's rhyme. Edwin woke, sweating, the word "No" croaking from his parched lips. He stood, unsteadily for a moment until the shaking subsided, then moved to his table. He sat for an age with a blank sheet of paper and his quill inked, before carefully marking the page into four and writing the names Beaumont, Allen, Weale, and Norris, one in each square.

Edwin stroked his unshaven chin as he worked, writing what he knew of each of the men in the relevant space. If a question occurred to him, he wrote it below his known facts. The process took him an hour and, when he finished, he smiled and nodded to himself.

The answer was clear.

But what to do about it?

Twenty Seven

Banging on the door below was followed by boots clattering up the stairs.

'Meg. Meg. Where are you?'

When I recognised Edwin's voice it occurred to me to lock myself in, to shout to him to leave. The thought flew away as quickly as it had arisen. If Edwin was in such a state, it must be important. I stepped out onto the landing. 'Here Edwin. What is it?'

'You must come with me.' He thrust out his hand. In it lay a small pistol. 'Take this, we may need it.'

I shook my head. 'No, Edwin. What makes you think I'd help you after what you said? I won't be used in that way.'

'I am a fool, Meg. And I think you know it.'

If he expected a soothing response from me, he got none. He also remained silent for a moment and his breathing slowed. What he said next was more considered. 'I apologise if I offended you. Honestly. It was not intended. They were words spoken in the heat of the moment, and worth nothing. I will not say you are indispensable - yet' the hint of a smile, 'but you are sharp, willing to learn, and courageous. And I need that courage now.'

Edwin held out the pistol again. This time I took it. 'But I can't use one of these.'

'It is simple, and you will only use it once.'

He showed me how to cock the hammer and to take aim. 'It is already primed and loaded. You will have one chance to take a shot if you need to, Meg. Keep it well away from your face. The man we are after has killed once and may not hesitate to kill again if he wishes to escape, so keep it trained on his heart.'

'Who is it?'

'Ralf Norris.'

I dropped against the landing wall. 'My mistress's brother? How -'

'I will explain later, Meg, but now we must go. If I miss him today, the magistrate may have arrested me tomorrow.'

Ralf Norris' house stood at the end of a terrace. Edwin sent me to guard the back, telling me to shoot Norris if he made a run for it, though I'd no confidence that I could do so if he did. I needn't have worried for Edwin soon opened the back door and beckoned me in.

Inside, Norris sat, head in his hands. A tear dropped from his cheek to his knee. Edwin gestured for me to stand beside him and train the pistol on our captive.

Edwin was the first to speak 'You know why we are

here, Ralf?'

The use of his first name told me Edwin wanted to keep him calm.

'I have been expecting you. Though you were hiding, I saw you in High Street and guessed you had spotted this.' He held up a glittering trinket of gold, with a long chain and a leaf design. It was the one Edwin had sent me to look for. 'I thought you had followed me there, so I did not turn back in case you had not seen the clasp.'

I was certain Edwin hadn't seen the item then, otherwise he'd have acted immediately.

He gave no hint when he spoke. 'It has taken me some time and trouble to discover you murdered Ben Steps. And now it is beyond doubt. What I am still unsure about is why.'

'It was an accident.'

'What I saw hardly looked an accident. The man's throat was cut.'

Norris' voice trembled. 'That was later.'

'Then I think you should tell it from the start. Did you decide to kill him when your sister told you about the stolen letters?'

Norris glanced up at Edwin. He looked perplexed that the thief-taker could know this.

'Surprised, Ralf? I told you I have put a lot of work into this murder. Continue.'

When Sarah told me what Steps was up to, I knew I must do something. Not murder, but something. Sarah and I have been close, always. When she was forced to marry Aubrey against her will, I moved to

Bridgnorth to make sure he treated her well. So far, he has been no worse than many husbands, better than some.

'My sister told me she feared that Steps would expose her if she did not pay, and I knew how this felt. Some years ago, I was the object of similar extortion. It was horrible and only ended when my torturer was chased from the town by a soldier and some of his friends who did not like his occupation.'

'And Steps tried again with you?'

Norris fell back against the wall, his arm out for support. 'No.'

'Well, he had your name on a list with others he was bleeding.'

'Then it must have been an intention, for he had not made any contact with me. God's teeth, I am even more glad he has gone than I was before.'

'Did Mrs Beaumont tell you where he lived?'

'She did not, only the man's name. I asked around but no-one seemed to know him. He clearly did not move in the same circles as me.'

'Then how did you find him?'

'I watched my sister and followed her when I could. One evening she left Cliffe House, clearly in disguise, and I knew what she was about. I kept my distance as she walked through the town and turned down Cartway. It was easy to stay back in the shadows down there and see which hovel she went into.'

'So, when she left Steps' home, you took your dagger, and set about ending your sister's misery.'

'No. That is not what happened.'

'How then?'

'I went only to reason with Steps. Despite what you might think, I am not a violent man. Naïve some might say, but not violent. It seemed to me he could be persuaded to give up what he had stolen. Sarah had already paid him all she could lay her hands on, so I thought if I offered him a reasonable sum Steps would release them. Instead, he came at me like a man possessed by the very devil, crying foul oaths and wielding a dagger. I thought him drunk because I easily side-stepped his first lunge but then he grabbed me. Before he could do me harm, I grasped his wrist, trying to shake the weapon from him. The next thing I knew, this madman pulled me to the floor with all his weight and we were rolling from side to side. A moment later, he screamed and clutched his neck. The dagger had pierced his throat and blood gushed from the wound.'

'You are asking me to believe it was an accident?'

Norris leant back in his chair. His confession had had spilled like a torrent but now the words flowed calmly. 'Only that part. His death was not an accident. I knew if Steps survived, he would wreak revenge on me, and more importantly, on Sarah. So, I took the blade from his shaking fingers and ripped open his throat with all my might. He gurgled for only a few seconds, then he was gone. As long as I live, I will never forget the look in his eyes. Nor the satisfaction I felt when I lifted him to his bed, unable to torture any more poor souls.

'Steps had Sarah's clasp pinned to his jerkin. I

recognised it straight away and knew he'd stolen it. It was my plan to get it back to her somehow when the dust had settled. So stupid of me to wear it in public.'

Edwin gestured for me to follow him outside. I glanced at Norris.

'He will not be going anywhere. Will you, Ralf?'

Norris shook his head slowly but did not speak.

'Come along, Meg, there is something I need you to do for me.'

Outside, Edwin leant against the wall.

'You know a man called Josephus Wellington?'

'A boatman?'

'The one. Go to him and tell him to be by the bridge at ten o'clock tonight, and that I have a cargo for him. Say he must bring provisions for at least five days. Now go, I must talk more to our friend in there, then I have arrangements to make. Meet me in front of your master's house when the bells strike eleven tomorrow.'

Twenty Eight

I'd spent the night wondering if Edwin would turn up at the house as he'd promised, or if he planned to escape in the dark, and was making sure I didn't give his game away. I should have trusted him. He arrived, grinning, on time, and told me Norris would now be well down river.

'You let him go?'

'Ralf Norris is not a criminal, Meg.'

'Yes he is. He killed a man, Edwin. He even admitted it.'

'Norris was forced to kill Steps to protect his sister. When he realised Steps had only been injured in their struggle, he knew the truth would come out unless he finished the job. Steps was evil, and it was only a matter of time before he met his end. To my mind justice has been done and Norris will be in Worcester by tonight. In two days, he will be boarding a ship in Bristol and within a month he will be starting a new life in the Americas. This is exile of a sort, and God knows what fate awaits him in that strange land.'

'What will Mr Beaumont say when he hears his

brother-in-law has gone? I doubt he'll even believe you.'

'He has no need to believe it. Because I am not going to tell him. As far as he will be concerned, we found the killer but he escaped, which, in a way, is true. I'll say I have no doubt the villain will be far away by now, and unlikely to return.'

'A convincing tale, Edwin, but I still think Mr Beaumont will see you hang.'

'There is no need to worry about that, Meg. Back me up when I tell him. Whether he takes it as the truth does not matter. By nightfall Beaumont will be in no position to harm me, nor his wife.'

So now I had to decide which path would benefit me most. If I went in to see my master at Edwin's side, and supported his story, I would lose my job without a doubt. But I would be trusted more by Edwin, and closer to my wish to follow in his footsteps. If I took my master's side, and exposed Edwin as a liar, I would lose any protection Edwin might offer. My chance of becoming a thief-taker would disappear like bonfire smoke in the wind. I could also take the middle road, refuse to go inside with him, so not put myself at risk with Mr Beaumont. Then Edwin would consider me a coward and be unwilling to act as my teacher.

I needed time to think on these choices. 'How did you work out Norris was the killer? It can't be because you saw the cloak clasp. That was before we argued about the possibilities.'

The grin came back to Edwin's face. 'Well, I did see it, but I did not realise I had.'

I must have looked puzzled, because I was.

'It is one of the tools we must never ignore, Meg. It is said that our dreams are portents of things to come, the spirit world communicating with us whilst we are asleep. I believe it may be so, but also that they are a way for us to make sense of things we have seen. Often that sense is difficult to grasp, but we can get to the nub if we think about it hard enough.'

'Sorry, Edwin, I still don't understand. What have dreams to do with this?'

'Two days ago, you and I disagreed badly. I said things I should not have said and hope you will forgive me. As a result of this, and other consternations, I took in more gin than I should. With these things combined, I dreamt I was being tried for Ben Steps' murder. I must have seen that cloak clasp on Ralf Norris in the town, because he was wearing it in my dream. It was quite clear, with its the golden leaves and glittering jewels, and it stayed with me when I woke. I thought I would need to work harder to have Norris admit what he had done, but his confession proves what I said, he is not an evil man.'

I could see the logic of Edwin's argument, and had to consider, again, if I trusted his judgement. It only took me a minute to decide. I swung my arm in an arc towards the house and followed him to the door.

The kitchen was the furthest I'd ever ventured inside my master's house before. Only then to warm by the fire on a cold winter's day, when cook had taken pity on me. This didn't happen often, but Mrs Garris was a kindly soul, a good cook, and a great teller of stories. One of these was how, when she was just a young assistant, the cook at the time, Mrs Nevin, was getting to the end of her days and handing out advice. She told Mrs Garris "Next year, you work on perfecting your simnel cake for Easter. Make one for all the servants and pass it round. I'd wager they'll say it is very good, but never as nice as Mrs Nevin's".

It seems the old cook laughed so much Mrs Garris thought she'd die then and there, but her prediction came true. 'You know, I did practice, over and over, and she was right, I never got it to be as good as hers.'

This time, I was to go through the front door, not the kitchen. Joseph tried to block my way, but Edwin gently pushed him aside, with a look saying not to try it again. The footman took the hint and hurried before us to open the door to the magistrate's room. Edwin didn't wait for his introduction.

'Good morning, Mr Beaumont.'

'Hare! Good God. What? Joseph - get that girl out of here.'

Joseph made a grab for me, and Edwin gave him that look again. He stopped, glanced at his master, then closed the door hard behind him as he dashed away.

Edwin folded his arms. 'She is with me, sir, and I wish her to stay so she may confirm what I will tell you.'

'Damn it, man, she is a servant in the garden.'

'In this matter Meg Valentine has been my

assistant and of great service, She *should* be in at the end of this.'

'The end? You have taken Steps' killer?'

'No.'

'Then -'

'Not taken. Unfortunately. But discovered. The finger finally came down on a journeyman rope-maker. He had been in Bridgnorth only a few months but had built up a feud with Steps over a debt. Young Meg here found it out.'

I stared at Edwin, but he ignored me and continued.

'We went to capture the man last night, but he heard we were coming and slipped away on a coal-barge travelling down river. I doubt we will see him again.'

My master laughed without humour. 'How convenient, Hare. I suppose you expect me to believe this cock-and-bull story and let you walk free?'

'You do not need to believe me, ask your servant, she will tell you the truth of it.'

'I would no more believe her than I do you. The girl has been trotting behind you, doing your bidding, since this whole affair began. Of course she will say anything you have asked her to.'

I stepped forward. 'Sir, I wouldn't do such a thing. What Mr Hare says is true -'

'Quiet, girl!' My master moved towards me and raised his hand to strike, but Edwin stood in his path.

'Lower your hand, sir, you will not beat Meg in my presence.'

'Then I will do it later. When the bailiff has taken you to his cells.'

'I would wager you will not have time, Mr Beaumont.' Edwin pointed to the clock. 'Within the hour, your name will be mud. Your history, your cruelty to your tenants, and your schemes to steal from your customers will all be public knowledge. I imagine the bailiff will be calling on you, not me.'

'What the -'

'You sent me out to find a murderer. You should not be surprised then, when I unearth more than you bargained for. It would be a shame to keep such juicy morsels to myself, would it not? I may have done, had you not threatened to try me for a crime you knew I had not committed. I didn't believe your customers would as forgiving as you imagined, so I had a printer produce a broadsheet. When the good citizens of Bridgnorth hear the truth of you, your word or your accusations will have no value. If I were you, I would pack away such goods as I could and escape as quickly as possible. For, make no mistake, you are a ruined man.'

My head spun. Not only had I lied for Edwin, but by doing so, I'd lost my livelihood. To leave my master's employ was one thing, to be seen as a servant not to be trusted was quite another. I wouldn't find work as a gardener anywhere in this town if the fact that I'd sided with Edwin came out.

Mr Beaumont looked this way and that, then slumped in his chair. Edwin put a hand on my shoulder and turned us towards the door. He whispered a few words to Joseph as we passed him in the entrance hall on our way out.

Twenty Nine

HBMS Denbigh

My dearest Sarah

By the time you read this I will be far off on my way to the Americas, and never likely to be with you again.

I do not know if Mr Hare has spoken to you of what occurred but for my own sanity I must confess to you of my part in the death of Ben Steps. Please believe that in the beginning it was a terrible accident, brought on by that evil man's assault on me, but then hot blood ran through my veins, and I had to finish him off so he could trouble you no more.

I have no regrets, other than having to leave you to defend yourself in this cruel world. I hope you will not need to do so alone for long. We both know your husband is a deceitful and dishonest man. He does not love you and you do not love him. I expect he will face his undoing before too many days have passed if what Mr Hare told me when he left me on the bank of the Severn is true.

Contrary to my initial impressions, Hare has shown

himself to be a good man, with your interests at heart, and I have observed you have some affection for each other. For your own sake, and that of your dear Hannah, leave Aubrey if you can, and make a new life with Edwin Hare.

These are just my simple words of advice, my lovely Sarah.

You will always be in my thoughts, the most precious sister a man could hope for.

Ralf

Thirty

Edwin was staring at a heavy sky when I arrived by The Swan. Four horses munched on hay, and the coachman checked wheels and baggage in preparation for a long day's journey north. The curtains of the carriage hid its passengers from curious glances, but I knew Mrs Beaumont would be inside.

'Looks like rain, Meg. Not a good day to set off, the roads to Carlisle can be treacherous even in summertime.'

I shrugged. 'I still don't see why you're leaving. My master has fled, leaving me out of work I might add, and everyone now knows you'd nothing to do with Ben Steps' death. There's a good living for you in Bridgnorth. How quickly will you get one where you're going?'

'You know it has little to do with what people think about me and Steps. Nor with money, though it may be difficult for a while. The problem is people like Quentin Goode. He will not be with us for much longer, but he knows something of my past life, and he unwittingly shared it with Steps. Who is to say he will not do the same again before he dies?'

'But Goode didn't do it on purpose.'

'No, you are right. He did it when he had a few drinks addling his brain. A man may say anything in those circumstances, I've done it myself, but if the things he knew come out, it would become very uncomfortable for me.'

I nodded towards the coach. 'Mrs Beaumont is travelling with you?'

'She and the child. Yes.'

'You're planning to set up home together?'

'Time will tell, Meg. Sarah managed to gather a few items of value before her husband's aggrieved customers came after him, so she will be comfortable for a while. Even that cloak clasp is worth a pretty penny. She can rent a house, not so grand as she is used to, but adequate for her needs. I will do the same nearby and we will see where our friendship goes. With Aubrey gone, Sarah has no need to take my lowly status into account, she will certainly now be no poorer with me than with him.'

The coachman rang a handbell and called for passengers to make themselves ready to leave. Edwin turned to climb aboard but I touched his forearm to hold him back.

'Can I ask you a question before you go, Edwin?'

'Of course.'

'What do you think will become of me? By joining with you, I put my future in your hands. I now have no work, and you are running away. Don't you care?'

The first spots of heavy raindrops began to fall, and the dark clouds seemed to be reflected on Edwin's face. 'You came to me willingly, Meg, did you not? You asked me to guide you in the skills of my trade, that of thief-taker. Have I fulfilled my side of the bargain?'

I sighed. 'You have.'

''And did you not work with me to find both a thief and a murderer, uncovering other secrets along the way?'

'I did.'

Edwin's dark expression lifted to form a smile. 'Then you have all the skills you need to make your way as a thief-taker, Meg Valentine. Begin small. I have made it clear to those who may have need of such services to seek you out. And they will. So only take the ones you think you can handle until you find your feet. This is how I started. Little by little, they will gain confidence in you, and you will find confidence in yourself.' He pulled a key from his pocket and passed it to me. 'In the meantime, I have paid the rent on my house for a half year, and you have use of it. On the table, you will find a box with enough to keep you from starvation for the next few months. I owe you that. When I am settled, I will send you an address and, if you feel the need, you can begin to repay me when you are able.'

Throughout this speech I stood open-mouthed, barely grasping his words, until, without waiting for a reply, Edwin raised his foot to the step, swung inside and pulled the door shut.

The curtains twitched aside as the coachman raised

his whip to coax the horses forward. Three faces smiled down, Edwin, Mrs Beaumont, and her child, Hannah, their waves continuing until the coach trundled under the Northgate.

I watched until they'd disappeared, then set off to begin the two jobs I needed to do. First was to find work which would allow me the freedom to become a thief-taker in my own right. The other was to find the dark-haired, brown-eyed, young man who had brought some lightness outside a dead man's door. I needed to ask him of his prospects.

A Word From The Author

My love of crime fiction goes way back to childhood and adolescence. Whether it be the Famous Five's criminal investigations, science fiction detectives on distant worlds, or Wilkie Collins' immortal *The Moonstone*, there is something fundamental in crime fiction. The unravelling of a mystery, the search for truth, and the thrill of the hunt. In good crime writing, there's also an examination of the human condition – a lone (and often flawed) protagonist struggling to bring order to the world in which they live.

I'm author of a series of crime novels featuring Inspector James Given, set in England and France in the late 1930s and early 1940s. I've also written a family saga, *A Handkerchief for Maria,* a novel based on research into my own family.

I now live near Ironbridge, Shropshire, the cradle of the Industrial Revolution. The *Meg Valentine Mysteries* series draws its inspiration from this area.

I hope you enjoyed reading *The Thief-Taker's Apprentice*, Follow my writing through the links below.

charliegarratt.com
charliegarratt.substack.com

Historical Note

The Thief-Taker's Apprentice is set in late 1749. King George II was on the throne and England was a very different place to now.

The mid-eighteenth century was on the cusp of industrialisation. For example, the Spinning Jenny, which revolutionised cotton production, didn't appear until 1764. The steam engine was still in it's infancy and wasn't applied to transport, like ships and railways, until later. Abraham Derby, who developed a coke burning blast furnace to produce cheaper pig iron, only succeeded in firing up the furnace in 1709.

At this time, there was no police force in England. The first was set up in London in 1829 by Sir Robert Peel. Up to then, locally appointed constables maintained the peace, but individuals were responsible for retrieving their own goods when stolen. This led to the rise of 'thief-takers', a kind of bounty hunter, who would be paid by victims or from government funds, to seek redress. The most infamous of these, Jonathan Wild, is immortalised in the novel *The History of the Life of the Late Mr. Jonathan Wild the Great* by Henry Fielding. Wild was accused of engaging his criminal friends to steal, and then giving them up to the authorities in order to claim the rewards.

Bridgnorth, the setting for *The Thief-Taker's Apprentice*, was an important port in the mid-eighteenth century, despite being over 70 miles from the sea. The River Severn was still navigable up to there. Some years later, the water meadows further up the river were reclaimed for farming, which increased the rise and fall of the flow, hence destroying Bridgnorth as a port. Much of the town, including its castle, was badly damaged in the English Civil War (1642-1651).

The eagle-eyed will have spotted the initials "HBMS" on the letter towards the end of the novel. A modern reader might have expected "HMS" i.e. "Her/His Majesty's Ship". In the eighteenth century these other initials were often used to denote "His Britannic Majesty's Ship".

If you enjoyed *The Thief-Taker's Apprentice,* please give it a review on Amazon or Goodreads this helps spread the word.

To hear about new releases from Charlie Garratt, please register at:
www.amazon.com/author/charliegarratt

Or click "Follow" at:
www.amazon.co.uk/stores/author/B0034NDJ78

Printed in Dunstable, United Kingdom